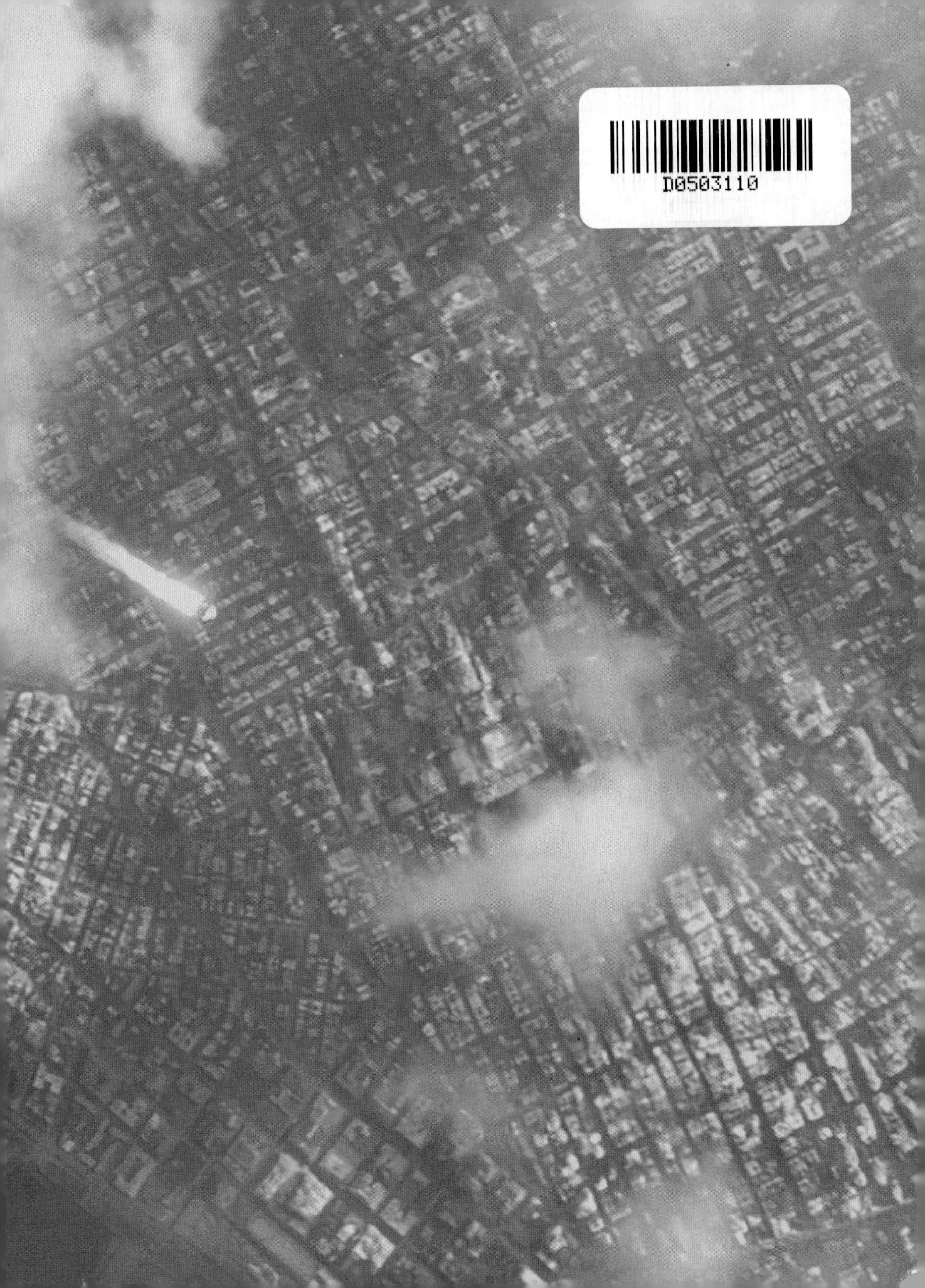

MARVEL STUDIOS

CHARACTER ENCYCLOPEDIA

Written by Adam Bray

CONTENTS

Welcome to a world where aliens invade, warlords plot, sorcerers cast spells, kings protect, and Avengers unite. Just who is trying to destroy this rich, complex universe—and who are the brave heroes joining forces to defend it?

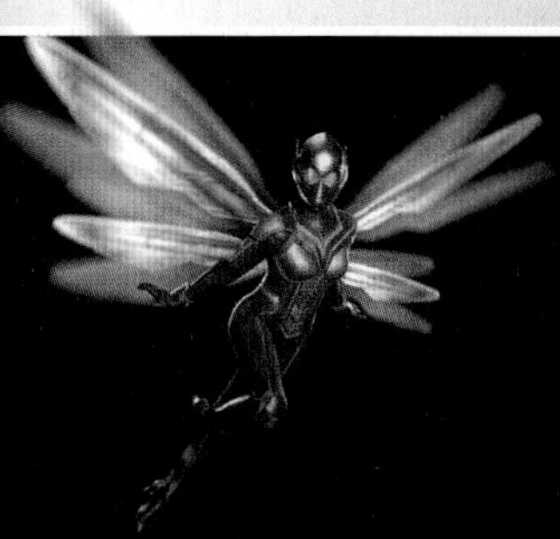

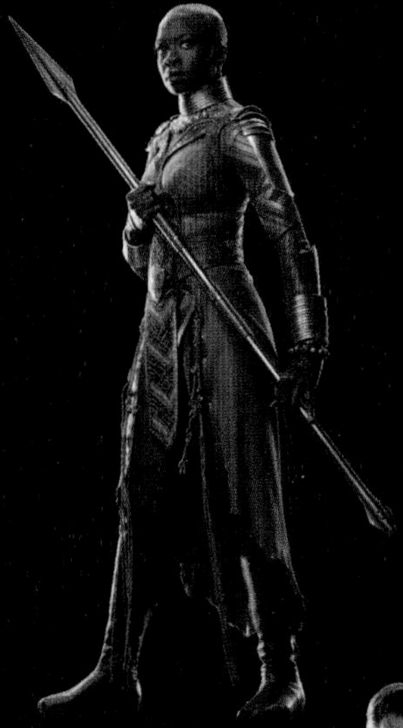

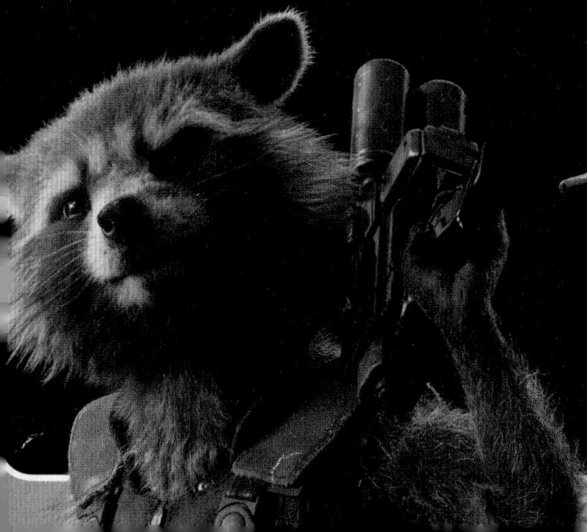

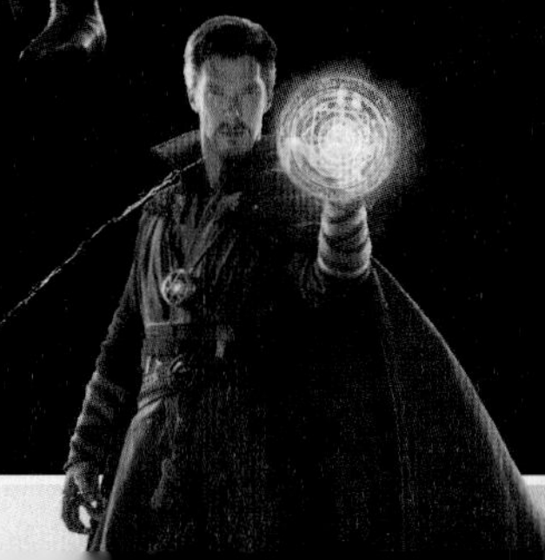

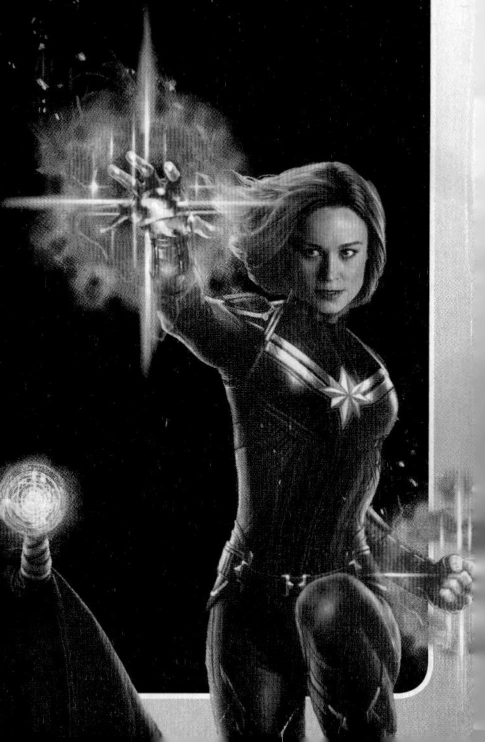

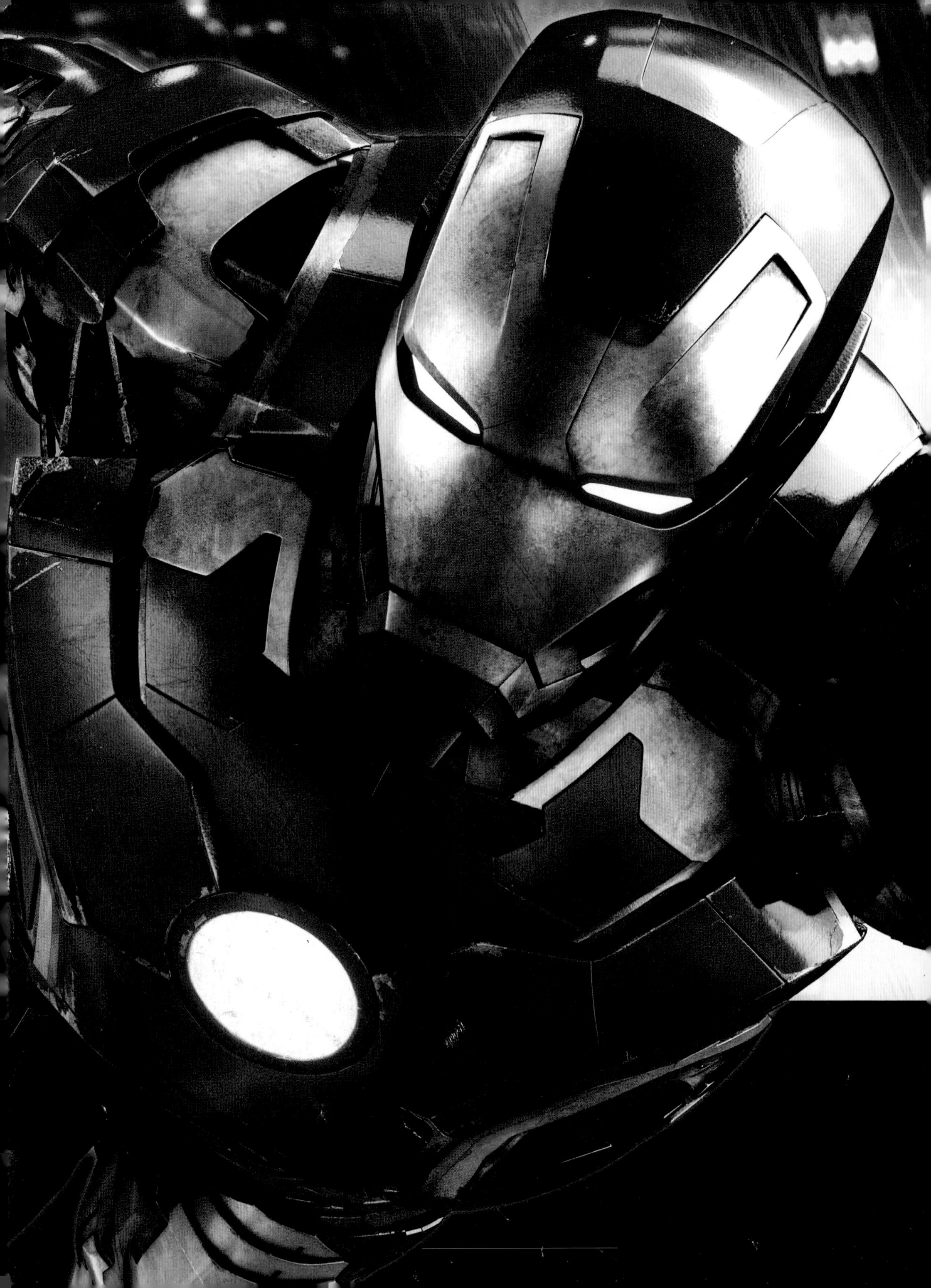

IRON MAN

Tony Stark is one of the world's wealthiest entrepreneurs. When he learns his tech company is a contributor to the world's problems, he finds new meaning in life as Iron Man. Wearing a high-tech, weaponized suit, Iron Man protects the world from terrorists and invaders.

TONY STARK

Genius billionaire inventor

Dr. Ho Yinsen saves Stark's life after a bomb injury. He helps build the prototype Iron Man armor to escape from the Ten Rings terrorists who hold them captive.

Tony Stark is the wealthy owner of Stark Industries. He initially makes his billions by selling weapons, but has a change of heart when he sees them used by extremists. He then resolves to use his multinational technology company to protect humanity and fund his team of super-powered heroes, the Avengers. He is engaged to Stark Industries' CEO, Pepper Potts.

Advanced RT (Repulsor Tech node) embedded in chest

METAL HEART

Stark's RT is a powerful electromagnet that keeps bomb shrapnel from Stark's old injury from reaching his heart. It also powers his Iron Man armor. The technology behind it was developed by Stark's father, Howard Stark, when he built a device called an Arc Reactor.

Casually dressed while at home

HIGH FLYER

Billionaire Tony Stark owns a customized Boeing 737, employing his own pilot and a sizable flight crew. After perfecting his Iron Man armor, he relies less on the plane, but still uses it for the occasional business trip to transport staff.

Stark secretly builds his Iron Man armor in the basement lab of his Malibu mansion.

IRON MAN

Armored Avenger

Tony Stark develops his first metallic suit of armor to escape the Ten Rings terrorist group in Afghanistan. Once home, Stark continues to develop ever more advanced versions of his Iron Man armor. As a founding member of the Avengers, he is always ready to suit up and fight any and all threats to humanity.

Entire helmet recedes via nanobots

Suit activated by RT

SUIT UP

Iron Man's Mark L armor uses nanotechnology to store itself inside Stark's chest-mounted RT (Repulsor Tech node). It instantly forms armor around him and includes several powerful new repulsor weapons.

Repulsor beam embedded in palm

New silver highlights

DARING RESCUE

Iron Man's repulsor technology easily penetrates the exterior of villain Ebony Maw's spacecraft. Iron Man races to rescue his allies Peter Parker and Doctor Strange.

DATA FILE

AFFILIATION: Stark Industries, Avengers
KEY STRENGTHS: Scientific genius, wealth, creativity. Iron Man: flight, strength, durability, missiles, repulsor beams
APPEARANCES: Iron Man, The Incredible Hulk, Iron Man 2, The Avengers, Iron Man 3, Avengers: Age of Ultron, Captain America: Civil War, Avengers: Infinity War

Stark solved an ice problem in his design early on, allowing him to even leave Earth's atmosphere.

Nanobots automatically repair surface damage

Upgraded high-speed thrusters

VIRGINIA "PEPPER" POTTS

Stark Industries CEO

As Tony Stark's personal assistant, Pepper Potts brings order to Tony's messy daily life. She even uncovers the treachery of his business partner, Obadiah Stane. Tony makes Pepper CEO of Stark Industries when he believes he is dying and she continues to manage everything while he combats Loki, Mandarin, and Thanos.

TIME OFF
Pepper and Tony fall in love, but his dangerous obsession with saving the world strains their relationship. They take a temporary break from each other for a while, but later get back together.

Fashionable business attire

Watch is a present from Tony Stark

IN CHARGE
Making Pepper CEO is one of the best decisions Tony Stark ever made, second only to asking her to marry him. Pepper is the only one who can handle his constant crises.

Grandmother's ring

DATA FILE
AFFILIATION: Tony Stark, Stark Industries, Happy Hogan

KEY STRENGTHS: Resourceful, independent, reliable, corporate leadership

APPEARANCES: Iron Man, Iron Man 2, The Avengers, Iron Man 3, Avengers: Infinity War

Pepper is infected with the dangerously unstable Extremis treatment by villain Aldrich Killian. Extremis allows Pepper to survive a fiery crash and blast Killian using an Iron Man repulsor.

HAROLD "HAPPY" HOGAN

Loyal bodyguard

Happy Hogan is Tony Stark's driver and bodyguard. After years of faithful service he is promoted, working for both Tony and Pepper Potts. Happy takes his job seriously, which leads him into the line of fire after investigating a suspicious figure, Eric Savin. After his recovery, Happy is entrusted with even greater responsibilities.

NEW NAME
Harold "Happy" Joseph Hogan earns his nickname because Tony Stark likes to tease him about his glum personality. Happy has a heart of gold, though, and considers Tony and Pepper his closest friends.

Strong and fit due to boxing training

Tailored suit reflects professional attitude

TAKING THE LEAD
Happy is a man of action. When he learns that Tony's nemesis Ivan Vanko and rogue rival Justin Hammer are up to no good, he races to Hammer Industries with no hesitation.

DATA FILE
AFFILIATION: Stark Industries, Tony Stark, Pepper Potts
KEY STRENGTHS: Loyalty, boxing, security expert, professional driver
APPEARANCES:
Iron Man, Iron Man 2, Iron Man 3

Happy is implicitly trusted by both Tony and Pepper, who promotes him to Stark Industries Security Chief.

Iron Man Mark V briefcase

COLONEL JAMES RHODES

Friend and patriot

Colonel James Rupert "Rhodey" Rhodes is an ace U.S. Air Force pilot in charge of purchasing gear from Stark Industries for the military. His relationship with his best friend Tony Stark is frequently tested by Stark's reckless behavior. However, Rhodey remains loyal to Stark and becomes a member of the Avengers.

Stark and Rhodes are best friends. Rhodey offers him pep talks when needed, but also plenty of tough love.

DATA FILE

AFFILIATION: U.S. Air Force, Tony Stark, Avengers
KEY STRENGTHS: Honor, duty, loyalty, military training, piloting. War Machine: flight, strength, missiles, guns, repulsor beams, sonic cannon
APPEARANCES: Iron Man, Iron Man 2, Iron Man 3, Avengers: Age of Ultron, Captain America: Civil War, Avengers: Infinity War

U.S. Air Force "Wings"

U.S. Air Force dress uniform

WHICH SIDE?
During the Avengers' Civil War—where the team disagree about whether to register their super-powers under the new Sokovia Accords legislation—Rhodey is unsure which side to choose.

BATTLE INJURY
Rhodes walks with a set of robotic leg braces after his back is broken during a battle between opposing factions of Avengers. He doesn't harbor a grudge, though.

WAR MACHINE

Weapon of war

War Machine is the codename used by Rhodey Rhodes when he wears Tony Stark's armor suits. Rhodey confiscates Stark's Mark II armor when his friend's irresponsible behavior gets out of hand, but Stark doesn't hold it against him. In fact, he upgrades the armor for Rhodey with all-new features.

Weapon storage compartment

NOT ENOUGH
Using high-tech braces that allow him to walk after a spinal injury, Rhodes dons the War Machine Mark IV armor in Wakanda. Despite Stark's best upgrades, however, the suit is no match for the warlord Thanos.

RT (Repulsor Tech node)

Hull pressure transducers

Wrist-mounted weaponry

Chromed titanium and steel exoskeleton

IRON MEN
Wearing his new War Machine suit, Rhodes joins his best friend, Tony Stark. Together they fight off Justin Hammer's drones before battling vengeful engineer Ivan Vanko.

Rhodes wears the War Machine Mark III armor during the Avengers' face-off at Leipzig-Halle Airport. Vision fires at Falcon, but accidentally hits Rhodes.

Repulsor jets in boots

At the Battle of Wakanda, War Machine fires at Thanos's charging army of Outrider soldiers.

RAZA HAMIDMI AL-WAZAR

Terrorist commander

Raza is the leader of a Ten Rings terrorist group that kidnaps Tony Stark in Afghanistan. He tries to force the captured Stark into building missiles for him, but Stark builds an Iron Man suit instead and escapes. Raza is secretly buying weapons from Stark's villainous business partner, Obadiah Stane, but unwisely tries to renegotiate the terms of the agreement with him.

DATA FILE

AFFILIATION: Ten Rings
KEY STRENGTHS: Terrorist resources, Stark Industries weapons
APPEARANCES: Iron Man

Devious mind full of nasty ideas

WRECKAGE

Raza and his men discover the wrecked armor of Stark's Iron Man prototype in the desert. They bring it back to camp but are unable to reassemble it.

Raza decides to use Stark's Iron Man armor as a bargaining tool with Obadiah Stane.

Hot coal

RAZA'S WEAKNESS

Raza isn't the head of Ten Rings—that's a shadowy figure known as the Mandarin. Raza is a well-educated lieutenant, rising through the ranks of the organization. His arrogance makes him blind to Tony Stark's escape plan.

British army camouflage

DR. HO YINSEN

Selfless surgeon

Dr. Ho Yinsen first met Tony Stark at a New Year's Eve party in Switzerland in 1999, though Stark doesn't remember. Yinsen is taken prisoner by Ten Rings and saves Stark's life when his heart is injured by a bomb. He helps Stark escape, knowing he can never actually leave himself.

INSPIRING MAN

Yinsen hails from Gulmira, Afghanistan. Though he leads a humble life and loses everything, he devotes himself to doing good. Yinsen encourages Stark to be a better man.

TRUE FRIEND

Yinsen helps Stark assemble his Iron Man prototype armor. When the computer operating system takes too long to upload, Yinsen creates a distraction to buy Stark more time.

Brilliant scientific mind

Tie maintains dignity in captivity

DATA FILE

AFFILIATION: Tony Stark

KEY STRENGTHS: Skilled doctor, scientist, multilingual

APPEARANCES: Iron Man, Iron Man 3

Tongs hold vessel of melted palladium

Yinsen has essential engineering skills, and builds parts for Tony's armor as well as a temporary electromagnet for his heart.

OBADIAH STANE

Double-dealing partner

When Tony Stark's parents died, Howard Stark's business partner, Obadiah Stane, stepped in as temporary CEO of Stark Industries. Stane mentored young Tony, who took over the company at age 21. Secretly, Stane has been resentful of Tony's inherited fortune all along and plots his demise.

Fine suit bought with Stark's money

CAN'T KEEP UP

Obadiah Stane helped Howard Stark and Anton Vanko create the original Arc Reactor, but the massive prototype seemed impractical to develop further. Stane is unable to duplicate Tony's mini version.

Pepper Potts discovers on Stane's computer that he betrayed Stark and has been plotting with terrorist group Ten Rings.

Pocket hides sonic stun device

Hidden away, Stane's engineers attempt to create an armor suit based on Stark's own.

Shoe specked with Afghan dust

BEWILDERED

Stark reveals the mini RT (Repulsor Tech node) embedded in his chest. Stane is secretly jealous of the achievement and frustrated that Tony won't share it with him.

IRON MONGER

Evil man of iron

Stane bases his Iron Monger suit on Stark's prototype armor, recovered by Ten Rings in Afghanistan. Trying to outdo Stark, Stane's engineers build a much larger suit, but it has a fatal flaw: Iron Monger freezes over at low temperatures.

DATA FILE

AFFILIATION: Stark Industries
KEY STRENGTHS: Deception, Stark Industries resources.
Iron Monger: strength, flight, Gatling gun, missile launcher
APPEARANCES: Iron Man

FINAL FIGHT

Pepper Potts enters Obadiah Stane's lab. She discovers he has already suited up as Iron Monger, ready to fight to the bitter end.

Head swivels back

Satellite phone and voice distortion

UNBALANCED

The Iron Monger hull is composed of Omnium steel with limbs controlled by powerful servo-hydraulics. The design focuses on smart weapons and targeting sensors over navigation.

RT stolen from Stark's chest

Arms can lift 15,000 lbs (6,804 kg)

PHIL COULSON
Agent and ally

Working at the heart of counter-terrorism intelligence agency S.H.I.E.L.D., under Director Nick Fury, Agent Philip J. Coulson is one of the secret organization's best operatives. Coulson is both likable and humble, despite his considerable authority within S.H.I.E.L.D. He assists Fury in recruiting the Avengers and integrating them into the team.

Encrypted
S.H.I.E.L.D. earpiece

DATA FILE
AFFILIATION: S.H.I.E.L.D., Avengers, Nick Fury
KEY STRENGTHS: Loyal, resourceful, devoted, steadfast, dedicated
APPEARANCES: Iron Man, Iron Man 2, Thor, The Avengers, Captain Marvel

SACRIFICE
Faithful to the end, Coulson gives his own life in an attempt to stop Loki's escape from the S.H.I.E.L.D. Helicarrier. Though unsuccessful, his sacrifice motivates the Avengers to work together.

MEETING A HERO
Phil Coulson is a big fan of Steve Rogers. He owns a set of original Captain America trading cards and even helps design Cap's new uniform. He is almost nervous when he first meets his hero.

Watch has sentimental value

Coulson is one of Nick Fury's best agents. He helps Fury manage Stark, Thor, and Steve Rogers.

NATALIE RUSHMAN

Undercover assistant

S.H.I.E.L.D. agent Natasha Romanoff is tasked with infiltrating Stark Industries and monitoring Tony Stark. She applies for a position in the legal department under the alias Natalie Rushman, and is soon promoted as Stark's personal assistant. Rushman eventually helps Stark defeat rival Justin Hammer and Ivan Vanko.

Secret agent Black Widow finally casts her false identity aside when she storms Hammer Industries.

DECEIVING LOOKS

Pepper Potts was concerned when Tony Stark requested Natalie Rushman as his new assistant, based mainly on her appearance. However, Rushman proves to be highly competent and a big help.

Hair styled to blend in among workforce

Manicured nails

Professional office wear

MASTER INFILTRATOR

Natalie Rushman skirts a line between being just provocative enough to keep Tony Stark's attention and stay close enough to monitor him, but without crossing any inappropriate romantic lines. Her mixed signals confuse Tony.

DATA FILE

AFFILIATION: Stark Industries, S.H.I.E.L.D., Tony Stark, Nick Fury
KEY STRENGTHS: Boxing and martial arts, spy skills, dedication
APPEARANCES: Iron Man 2

JUSTIN HAMMER

Corporate rival

Hammer Industries is run by Justin Hammer, one of Tony Stark's biggest competitors. The inept CEO isn't capable of innovating anything successful himself. Instead, he steals corporate secrets from his rivals. Hammer tries to force engineer Ivan Vanko to duplicate Stark's Iron Man technology, but, as always, his plan fails.

Glasses worn solely to look smart

Single-breasted three-piece suit with notched lapel

Oversize tie indicates gaudy sense of style

UPSET PLAN

Hammer's plan to steal Stark's tech backfires disastrously. Instead of building suits of armor like Hammer asks, Vanko builds robotic drones—all under his own control. Then he turns against Hammer, leaving him to face the legal consequences.

Hammer is in Monaco for a TV interview. But when the interviewer chooses to follow a story about Tony Stark instead, Hammer is furious.

DEFECTIVE HARDWARE

Hammer boasts a success over his rival when he takes over Stark's military contracts. However, nothing that Hammer installs actually functions correctly in battle.

DATA FILE

AFFILIATION: Hammer Industries, Seagate Prison, Ivan Vanko
KEY STRENGTHS: Manipulation, thievery, ambition
APPEARANCES: Iron Man 2

WHIPLASH

Ivan Vanko

Ivan Vanko's father, Anton, helped Howard Stark invent the first Arc Reactor. But when Anton tried to sell the technology out from under Stark, he was deported, ending up in a Russian prison and living the rest of his life destitute. Ivan uses the technology to create a "Whiplash" suit and seek revenge on Howard's son, Tony Stark.

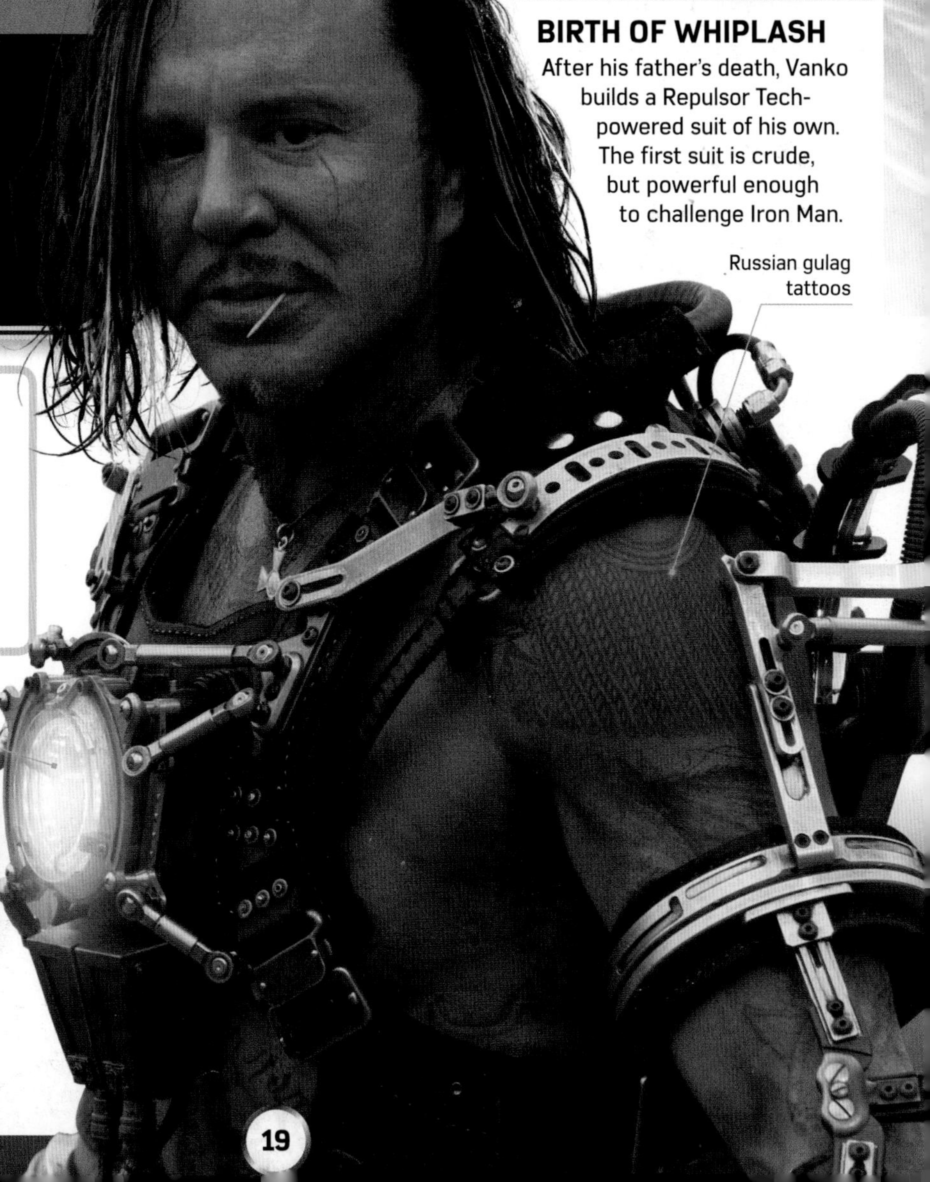

Unkempt hair
Russian gulag tattoos
External miniature RT (Vanko version)

DATA FILE

AFFILIATION: Hammer Industries, Anton Vanko

KEY STRENGTHS: Engineering genius. Whiplash suit: electro-whips, strength, flight

APPEARANCES: Iron Man 2

WHIPPED INTO SHAPE

Vanko's RT (Repulsor Tech node) channels energy to a pair of hand-held electro-whips that are connected to his suit. They are strong enough to cut through most metals and even deflect Iron Man's powerful energy blasts.

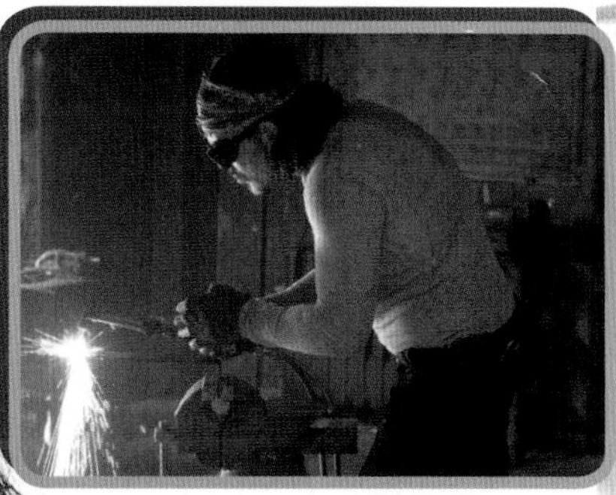

BIRTH OF WHIPLASH

After his father's death, Vanko builds a Repulsor Tech-powered suit of his own. The first suit is crude, but powerful enough to challenge Iron Man.

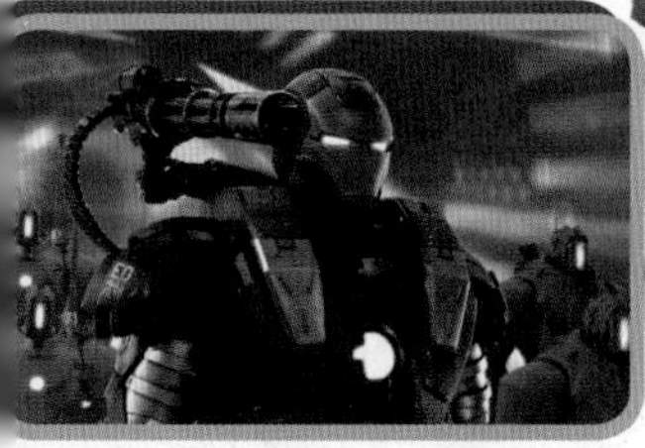

Vanko bides his time, waiting to attack Stark. He hacks into War Machine's suit, using it to attack Stark.

CHRISTINE EVERHART

Rising journalist

Gutsy reporter Christine Everhart pursues stories about Stark Industries' shady business dealings—including those with Ten Rings. Everhart has both professional and romantic interests in Tony Stark, which leads to awkward confrontations. Later, she becomes a TV news anchor and covers stories about the Avengers.

Everhart tips Stark off that his company's weapons were used to bomb the village of Gulmira, Afghanistan.

HIGH PROFILE

Everhart is an ambitious journalist, working for Vanity Fair and WHIH World News. In addition to Tony Stark and rival businessman Justin Hammer, her interviewees include President Ellis and ex-con-turned-Avenger Scott Lang.

Professional attire

Digital recording device

DATA FILE

AFFILIATION: WHIH World News, Vistacorp, Vanity Fair, Tony Stark
KEY STRENGTHS: Ambition, persistence, strategy
APPEARANCES: Iron Man, Iron Man 2

MONACO MEETING

Everhart follows CEO Justin Hammer to Monaco to interview him for Vanity Fair. After they bump into Tony Stark, she loses interest in Hammer, abandoning him to cover a story about Stark.

MATTHEW ELLIS

President of the United States

ENEMIES UNKNOWN

President Ellis previously banned the scientific research of Advanced Idea Mechanics (A.I.M.), an organization run by the shadowy Aldrich Killian. Killian plans to take revenge against Ellis by assassinating him and taking control of the White House.

Well-tended hair for cameras

Following a series of explosions that are blamed on a terrorist known as the Mandarin, President Matthew Ellis steps up. He rebrands military hero War Machine as the Iron Patriot and orders him to hunt down the Mandarin. Ellis, however, is unaware that a former acquaintance of his, Aldrich Killian, is the true terrorist.

Finely tailored suit

BAD PUBLICITY

Killian's bodyguard, Eric Savin, kidnaps President Ellis by placing him inside the Iron Patriot armor and flying him back to Killian. Killian intends to assassinate Ellis on TV.

Shure SM57VIP dual microphones

DATA FILE

AFFILIATION: U.S. government
KEY STRENGTHS: Authority of the Presidency
APPEARANCES: Iron Man 3

ALDRICH KILLIAN

Extreme enemy

A disabled and socially-awkward Aldrich Killian met Tony Stark in 1999, hoping to discuss his research agency A.I.M., but Stark brushed him off. Years later, Killian teams up with scientist Maya Hansen to develop her Extremis treatment, using it to heal his body. He covers up Extremis's explosive side-effects using a fake villain named Mandarin.

Well-groomed hair

Custom-tailored suit

Rings are valuable and unusual

Body has regenerated following Extremis treatment

Killian explains Extremis to Pepper Potts, hoping to gain Stark Industries' support for his experimental research.

HOT UNDER THE COLLAR

Extremis reprograms human DNA to heal the body rapidly, repairing injuries, curing disease, regrowing lost limbs, and improving overall physical performance. Adverse effects include uncontrollable heat radiation and explosions. Killian can even breathe fire.

LAST STAND

Aldrich Killian and Tony Stark fight aboard Killian's oil tanker, *Norco*. With Extremis active in his system, Killian is a formidable adversary.

Expensive, fancy shoes

MAYA HANSEN

Extremis inventor

Maya Hansen is the genetics genius who created Extremis, a treatment that rewrites DNA to heal injuries. Unfortunately, Extremis has a terrible side effect where most recipients rapidly heat up and sometimes explode. Hansen tries to partner with Tony Stark in 1999, but when he ditches her, she works with Aldrich Killian instead.

CONFLICTED

Maya Hansen is driven to create Extremis by the desire to help people. She partners with Killian for funding, even though she knows he is in it for the wrong reasons. Hansen finally sides with Tony Stark, but by then it is too late.

SECRET LAIR

As part of Killian's research agency, A.I.M., Hansen conducts her research in a secret lab with 40 scientists and a handful of test subjects.

Arms crossed defensively

Casual attire makes her appear unthreatening

Hansen gains Pepper Potts's confidence by pretending to betray Killian, but it's actually a ruse to kidnap Potts.

ERIC SAVIN

Enhanced bodyguard

DATA FILE

AFFILIATION: A.I.M., Aldrich Killian, Mandarin

KEY STRENGTHS: Generates extreme heat, rapid regeneration, enhanced strength

APPEARANCES: Iron Man 3

Retired Lieutenant Colonel Eric Savin is injected by Aldrich Killian with the Extremis treatment to heal his war injuries. He works as Killian's bodyguard and suits up in Rhodey Rhodes's stolen Iron Patriot armor to board Air Force One and kidnap the President. Savin meets his end fighting an Iron Man drone.

Focused mind keeps Extremis in check

HOTHEAD

The Extremis treatment inside Savin allows him to heal instantly after an injury—he can even regrow a foot! Extremis also causes him to generate massive internal heat.

MULTITASKER

As Killian's right-hand man, Savin has many duties, including coordinating covert missions for the other Extremis candidates. He also leads a helicopter assault that completely destroys Tony Stark's Malibu mansion.

Body has elevated temperature

Savin crosses paths with Stark's bodyguard, Happy Hogan.

MANDARIN
Trevor Slattery

Trevor Slattery is a failed British actor. He is hired by criminal mastermind Aldrich Killian to pose as a terrorist known as Mandarin, leader of the Ten Rings. Slattery creates videos taking credit for explosions that are actually caused by Killian's genetic treatment, Extremis. Slattery is caught and sent to prison, where he is kidnapped by the real Mandarin.

Long hair in bun

Gaudy costume jewelry rings

TELEVISION MENACE
The Mandarin rambles on in his videos, not making a lot of sense, but it sounds terrifying. His real purpose isn't to convey a specific ideology. He doesn't even know what he's saying—or that the public thinks he is real!

DARK
In addition to his flamboyant Asian costume, the Mandarin uses shadows and sunglasses to appear mysterious and frightening.

The Mandarin uses a mixture of Eastern symbols and violence in his video backdrops.

DATA FILE
AFFILIATION: A.I.M., Seagate Prison, Ten Rings (fake)
KEY STRENGTHS: Acting
APPEARANCES: Iron Man 3

IRON PATRIOT

Stars and stripes

Tony Stark creates a new armor suit and gives it to his friend Rhodey Rhodes to replace his War Machine Mark I armor. This new War Machine Mark II armor is then painted red, white, and blue, and rebranded as Iron Patriot by the U.S. Air Force to sound less threatening.

Cannon sits on articulated arm

Retractable face plate

Weaponry concealed in wrists

UNPATRIOTIC PLOT
Iron Patriot is given the task of hunting down the terrorist known as the Mandarin, but he is lured into a trap by the sinister Aldrich Killian. Killian kidnaps Rhodey and steals his armor.

"FF" stands for First Fighter Wing

Stabilizer belt balances armor during flight

Killian's henchman, Eric Savin, wears the Iron Patriot armor and boards Air Force One to kidnap the President.

Palms fitted with repulsors

DATA FILE
AFFILIATION: U.S. Air Force, Tony Stark
KEY STRENGTHS: Flight, strength, missiles, minigun, machine gun, repulsor beams, sonic cannon
APPEARANCES: Iron Man 3

Thruster boots controlled by A.I. system

DISARMING
Rhodes's new armor is an improvement on his old armor. However, it has been modified by A.I.M., Aldrich Killian's research agency. The U.S. Air Force trusts Killian, unaware of his plan to kidnap the President.

HARLEY KEENER

Young ally

Harley Keener lives with his mother in Rose Hill, Tennessee. One night, he encounters a distressed Tony Stark in his garage, trying to mend his broken Iron Man armor. Keener helps Stark and shows him around town. The boy gets caught up in a fight between Tony Stark and dangerous villain Eric Savin, but breaks free with Stark's help.

Button-up shirt for school

BUDDING SCIENTIST

Though Stark departs without much of a goodbye, he appreciates Keener's help. Stark sends the boy a haul of robots, computers, science equipment, and a new potato gun.

Backpack full of books and potatoes

UNLIKELY FRIENDS

Keener helps Tony Stark find the site of an explosion where a local man, Chad Davis, died. He then takes Stark to meet Davis's mother at a local bar. Keener's support helps Stark uncover part of a dangerous conspiracy.

Keener is a temporary custodian of Stark's Iron Man Mark XLII armor while it recharges in his garage.

Sneakers nearly outgrown

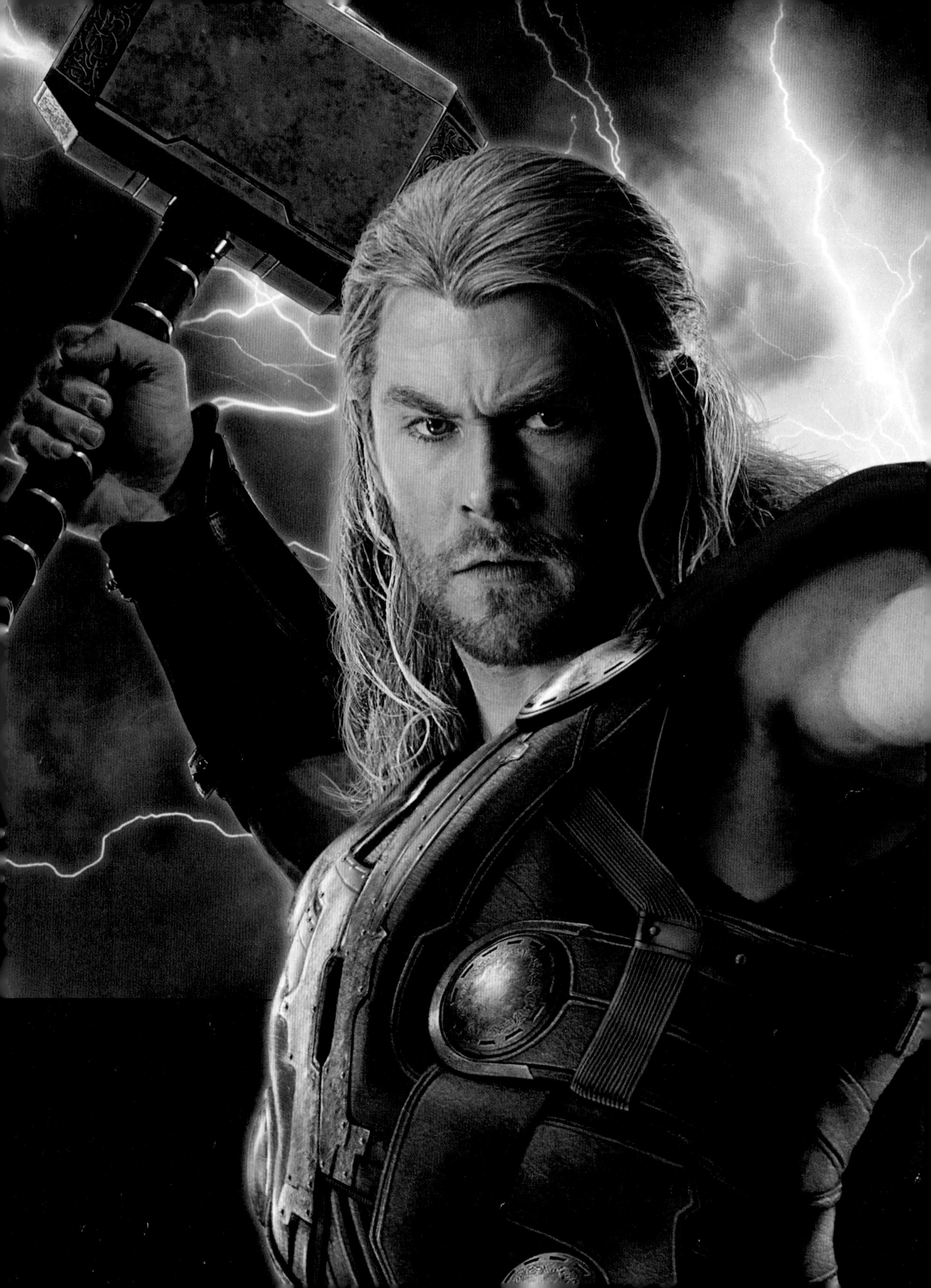

THOR

Asgard is home to brothers Thor and Loki. They quarrel for control of their kingdom, but find themselves facing foes from other planets, worlds, and dimensions. Thor and Loki must overcome their rivalry to protect their allies, citizens, and even Asgard itself.

THOR

God of Thunder

Thor is the eldest son of Odin and Frigga, the king and queen of the realm of Asgard. After a brief exile on Earth, Thor joins the Avengers. Upon the passing of his father, Thor becomes king of Asgard, although his world is destroyed by Surtur the Fire Demon.

Royal disks of Asgardian Realms

Mjolnir

MIGHTY MJOLNIR

Thor's enchanted hammer, Mjolnir, was forged in the heart of a dying star. It can only be wielded by someone who is deemed worthy. When Mjolnir is destroyed by Hela, Thor asks the Dwarf King Eitri to forge a new hammer called Stormbreaker.

Steel bracers protect arms

Leather and steel armor

Scale armor

FIGHTING FOR EARTH

At the Battle of New York, Thor joins forces with Captain America and the Avengers to stop his brother Loki and the alien Chitauri invasion.

Thor can wield lightning without his hammers, but they focus the lightning's power.

Leather boots

DATA FILE

AFFILIATION: Asgard, Avengers, Loki, Dr. Jane Foster

KEY STRENGTHS: Strength, agility, near-invulnerability, can summon lightning, power of Mjolnir and Stormbreaker

APPEARANCES: Thor, The Avengers, Thor: The Dark World, Avengers: Age of Ultron, Thor: Ragnarok, Avengers: Infinity War

LOKI
God of Mischief

Loki is the adopted son of King Odin and Queen Frigga of Asgard. His biological father, King Laufey, ruler of the Frost Giants, abandoned Loki soon after his birth. Loki is jealous of his older brother Thor. He uses trickery to steal the throne for a time. Although he rebels against his family, Loki later helps Thor save their people from the dangerous Hela.

Emotionless face hides deception

Scuffed bronze armor plating

TRICKSTER
Loki learns Asgardian Magic from his mother Frigga. His favorite magic tricks—mostly used for personal gain—include creating doppelgängers (identical copies of himself), changing his or others' appearance, and moving objects with his mind.

Hand reaches for concealed dagger

DATA FILE
AFFILIATION: Asgard, Thor, Thanos, Chitauri invaders, Grandmaster
KEY STRENGTHS: Magic, long life, rapid regeneration, deception
APPEARANCES: Thor, The Avengers, Thor: The Dark World, Thor: Ragnarok, Avengers: Infinity War

Loki wields the Mind Stone in his scepter, allowing him to control minds. It is one of six Infinity Stones, powerful objects that are sought after across the Multiverse.

BROTHERS IN ARMS
Thor releases Loki from prison so that they may join forces and avenge their mother, save Dr. Jane Foster, and defeat the Dark Elf Malekith.

Coat lined with green silk

Leather Asgardian boots

ODIN

King of Asgard

Patch over eye lost in battle

Odin is the wise and powerful all-father, ruler of Asgard. His wife is Frigga and his children are Hela, Thor, and Loki. Odin is known for being stern, but there is always a good reason for his strong-willed decrees. Though he is tough on his sons, and Loki rebels against him, Odin loves them both.

Royal disks

Odin sits on his throne wielding the spear Gungnir. It has power over Asgard, including the Bifrost bridge and the Destroyer.

Folded hands convey confidence and quiet authority

Gold woven into tunic fabric

ASGARD SACKED

Odin surveys the damage after Asgard is ransacked by the Dark Elves. Grieving the loss of his wife, Odin locks down his kingdom.

Ceremonial royal Asgardian cape

FINAL REST

After he is stranded on Earth by Loki, Odin spends his last days in Norway with the aid of the sorcerer Doctor Strange. Upon bidding farewell to his sons, Odin joins his wife Frigga in Valhalla, the Asgardian afterlife.

DATA FILE

AFFILIATION: Asgard
KEY STRENGTHS: Leadership, strength, long life, power of Gungnir
APPEARANCES: Thor, Thor: The Dark World, Thor: Ragnarok

FRIGGA

Queen of Asgard

Thor and Loki's loving mother Frigga is devoted to her family. She speaks up for Thor during his exile. Even when Loki tries to seize the throne and ends up in prison, she visits him and also pleads his case to her husband Odin. Though Odin refuses to release Loki, Frigga trusts he has a plan.

Radiant gemstones from Vanaheim

A proud mother, Frigga stands beside Loki during Thor's coronation ceremony, before it is interrupted by thieving Frost Giants.

Traditional Asgardian knot patterns

FAMILY PROTECTOR

Frigga is a highly skilled swordfighter. She faces Malekith, leader of the Dark Elves, when he invades the palace. Frigga sacrifices herself to protect Thor's girlfriend, Dr. Jane Foster.

Royal gown for Thor's coronation

Green represents new beginnings

MAGICAL MOTHER

Frigga is a sorceress. She teaches Magic to her younger son Loki to give him a competitive edge in battle.

DATA FILE

AFFILIATION: Asgard
KEY STRENGTHS:
Magic, selfless love, swordfighting
APPEARANCES: Thor, Thor: The Dark World

33

LADY SIF

Asgardian powerhouse

Lady Sif is one of Asgard's greatest warriors. She is a close friend of Thor and the Warriors Three. She aids Thor during his exile and helps him escape from Asgard to fight the Dark Elves. Lady Sif is not present on Asgard during the Ragnarok destruction, thus surviving the calamities that befall her people.

Toughened Asgardian steel

MYSTICAL BLADE

Sif's magical sword can extend into a double-bladed spear. The sword locks together with her shield and can be carried on her back. The sword is reforged after it is badly damaged while fighting the Destroyer.

Sword hilt

Overlapping armor plates provide flexible protection

Shirt of chain mail beneath armor

Bracer holds wrist wrap in place

Leather and chain mail skirt

MOUNTED COMBAT

Sif rides to war against pirate hordes on her mighty steed. A much-honored fighter, her horse is kept for her in the royal stables on Vanaheim.

Sif has feelings for Thor, but she hides them in case they spoil their friendship.

Sif fights invading Marauders alongside Thor and the army of Asgard after the Bifrost is destroyed.

DATA FILE

AFFILIATION: Asgard, Thor, Warriors Three
KEY STRENGTHS: Strength, speed, agility, hand-to-hand combat
APPEARANCES: Thor, Thor: The Dark World

HEIMDALL

Guarding the bridge

Heimdall is stationed at an observatory on the edge of Asgard's famed Rainbow Bridge. Here he guards the Bifrost, Asgard's gateway to the Nine Realms. Heimdall has the ability to see into the far reaches of the universe and allow others, such as his best friend Thor, to see through his eyes, too.

Intimidating bull horns-shaped helm

LOYALTY AND HONOR

Heimdall shows steadfast allegiance to Asgard's throne, and he defends his people to the death. He isn't afraid to break the rules, though, if there is a good enough reason.

Heavy armor protects from Bifrost energy

Bronze bracers on forearm

MAGIC SWORD

Heimdall uses his sword, Hofund, to lock or unlock the Bifrost from his observatory. (Odin's spear can open the Bifrost as well.) In special circumstances, Hofund can be used to activate the gateway from anywhere.

Sword is 5ft 4 in (1.6 m) long

Soft ox leather leggings

DATA FILE

AFFILIATION: Asgard

KEY STRENGTHS: Strength, sword fighting, long life, infinite sight, Bifrost control

APPEARANCES: Thor, Thor: The Dark World, Thor: Ragnarok, Avengers: Infinity War

Heimdall is exiled from Asgard by Loki (who is disguised as Odin). Loki is afraid Heimdall will see through his facade.

VOLSTAGG

Valiant warrior

Volstagg is a friend of Thor and, alongside comrades Fandral and Hogun, is one of the fabled Warriors Three. Lady Sif is the fifth member of their close-knit circle. A loyal companion, Volstagg readily comes to Thor's aid when he is exiled and helps battle the Destroyer. Volstagg is finally defeated by the vengeful Hela.

Long hair is typical of Asgardian warriors

Battle-worn pauldron

Hauberk (chain mail shirt)

VOLSTAGG THE VICTORIOUS

Volstagg is one of Asgard's greatest warriors. There are legendary tales of his battles across the Nine Realms after the Bifrost bridge was destroyed.

READY AND ABLE

Volstagg has a big heart, but poor judgment. He readily joins Thor and his friends on many misadventures, including an invasion of Jotunheim.

Forearm armor

Separate bracer for greater range of motion

Volstagg has a huge appetite. In truth, he savors victory banquets as much as the actual victory.

Etched steel battle ax

DATA FILE

AFFILIATION: Asgard, Thor, Sif, Warriors Three
KEY STRENGTHS: Strength, stamina, loyalty
APPEARANCES: Thor, Thor: The Dark World, Thor: Ragnarok

KING LAUFEY

King of the Frost Giants

King Laufey led his army of Frost Giants in an invasion of Tønsberg, Norway, in 965 CE. Odin and the forces of Asgard engaged them in battle, forcing them back to their homeworld on Jotunheim, and defeating them there. Laufey signed a peace treaty and gave Odin his weapon of mass destruction, the powerful Casket of Ancient Winters.

"Crown" made from jade stone

Laufey and the Frost Giants hide among the icy ruins of Jotunheim, where they look like part of the bleak landscape.

Blue skin is ice-cold to the touch

DATA FILE

AFFILIATION: Jotunheim, Frost Giants, Loki

KEY STRENGTHS: Can form ice at will or freeze anything on contact

APPEARANCES: Thor

THE END OF PEACE

When Thor and his friends invade Jotunheim, Odin intervenes to restore the peace treaty between himself and Laufey. It is too late, however: Laufey promises war.

Scarification designs indicate rank

LOKI'S REVENGE

Laufey is Loki's biological father, who abandoned his son for being too small. Loki was raised instead by Odin. Years later, Loki tricks Laufey into invading Asgard. He then eliminates Laufey to save adoptive father Odin.

DR. JANE FOSTER

Leading astrophysicist

Brilliant young scientist Dr. Jane Foster is one of the world's foremost astrophysicists and astronomers. She encounters Thor when he is banished to Earth and the two quickly fall in love. Foster helps Thor to both redeem himself and save the universe from the Dark Elf Malekith and his apocalyptic weapon, the Aether.

FLEETING LOVE

Thor and Jane Foster's romance is made difficult by Thor's long absences. Facing danger on a regular basis is also a lot for anyone to handle. As a result, Jane ends their relationship after a violent battle in Sokovia.

Notebook on Bifrost phenomenon

MYTHOLOGICAL MOMENT

Thor and Jane share a moment on the rooftop of her New Mexico lab. Foster develops greater trust in Thor after he teaches her about the Nine Realms of Asgard.

Foster is one of the first to believe Thor when he appears on Earth. She drives him to find his hammer.

Winter jacket

Foster slaps Loki when she finally meets him on Asgard, though he later ends up saving her life when they confront Malekith.

Winter-proof hiking boots

DATA FILE

AFFILIATION: Thor, Dr. Selvig, Culver University, Darcy Lewis
KEY STRENGTHS: Scientific mind, bravery, determination
APPEARANCES: Thor, Thor: The Dark World

DR. ERIK SELVIG

Scientist

Brilliant theoretical physicist Dr. Erik Selvig is a mentor of Jane Foster and a friend of Thor's. He is hired by S.H.I.E.L.D. to study the Tesseract, a mysterious relic, but Thor's rebellious brother Loki takes control of Selvig's mind, temporarily frazzling his personality. Selvig later accepts a job with the Avengers.

Tie borrowed from junior intern, Ian Boothby

Loki's mind control took its toll on Selvig. Darcy Lewis checks him out of a mental hospital after he is caught running around naked.

Thrift store second-hand jacket

Bag contains scientific equipment

NEW RESEARCH
Dr. Selvig and intern Darcy Lewis work with Jane Foster in their rented office space in New Mexico. Their chance encounter with Thor leads them to debate all things Asgardian.

CLUED IN
Selvig's theoretical work on the existence of other worlds makes him the perfect ally for Thor when the Asgardian finds himself on Earth.

Selvig works on the top-secret Project P.E.G.A.S.U.S., studying the Tesseract. His aim is to unlock the power of this mystical object.

DATA FILE

AFFILIATION: Thor, Dr. Jane Foster, Darcy Lewis, Loki, S.H.I.E.L.D., Avengers

KEY STRENGTHS: Genius, expert knowledge of Asgardian mythology

APPEARANCES: Thor, The Avengers, Thor: The Dark World, Avengers: Age of Ultron

DARCY LEWIS

Resourceful intern

Jane Foster and Erik Selvig are lucky to have an intern as smart and devoted as Darcy Lewis. She stays with them during the chaos of Thor's banishment on Earth. She manages to free Selvig from a mental hospital and, with the aid of her own intern, Ian Boothby, helps defeat the Dark Elves during their invasion.

Burgundy beanie hat

Fashionable scarf

Phone keeps Darcy in the know

STUDENT LIFE
Darcy is a student of political science. She is receiving six college credits for her internship with Jane Foster and Erik Selvig. The job proves to be far different to what she initially expected.

Darcy greets Thor, who arrives barely minutes after Jane Foster's reappearance through a wormhole.

Grey wool toggle jacket

PILLAR OF THE TEAM
Darcy works tirelessly for Jane Foster and Erik Selvig, without any pay. She keeps them grounded in the real world as they debate Thor's story and the existence of Asgard.

DATA FILE
AFFILIATION: Thor, Dr. Jane Foster, Dr. Erik Selvig, Ian Boothby
KEY STRENGTHS: Ingenuity, takes initiative
APPEARANCES: Thor, Thor: The Dark World

IAN BOOTHBY

The intern

BUDDING SCIENTIST

Ian has a strong scientific background. He has an interest in ornithology, and studies astronomy and physics in grad school. He hopes to follow in Dr. Foster's footsteps and become a leading scientist.

Simple winter cap

Jane Foster's phase meter

Second-hand cargo pants

Ian Boothby is an unpaid intern who assists Darcy Lewis, the intern of Dr. Jane Foster. The London university student is working for Lewis when they discover a strange network of inter-dimensional portals leading to Svartalfheim, homeworld of the vengeful Dark Elves. Ian helps Darcy find Dr. Selvig when Jane Foster leaves, and then does all he can to help thwart the Dark Elves.

RUNNING OUT OF TIME

Ian and Darcy hammer gravimetric spikes into the ground in Greenwich, England. They watch as the leader of the Dark Elves, Malekith, arrives and battles Thor.

DATA FILE

AFFILIATION: Darcy Lewis, Dr. Erik Selvig, Dr. Jane Foster
KEY STRENGTHS: Helpful, enthusiastic, loyal
APPEARANCES: Thor: The Dark World

Ian is a quiet yet helpful intern, willing to help where he can. He poses as Selvig's son to free him from custody, and later saves Darcy's life.

Hiking boots

DESTROYER

Vault guardian

The warden of Odin's vault is known as the Destroyer. The robot-like sentry has no mechanical parts. It is a magical armored soldier charged with protecting Odin's most valuable weapons and dealing retribution upon the all-father's enemies. When the Destroyer attacks Thor on Earth, it is vanquished with the power of the Thunder God's hammer, Mjolnir.

Internal furnace burns with Odinforce

"Eyes" open to emit deadly blasts

Magically transforming metallic body

CONTROLLED REMOTELY
The Destroyer is controlled by Gungnir, the spear of the king of Asgard. The Destroyer will obey anyone who wields Gungnir, including Loki when he takes the throne.

Virtually indestructible armor

DESTROYER UNLEASHED
The Destroyer arrives on Earth under the control of Loki, with a mission to eliminate Thor. Lady Sif and the Warriors Three try to stop him, without success.

DATA FILE
AFFILIATION: Asgard, Odin, Loki
KEY STRENGTHS: Strength, near invincibility, energy blasts
APPEARANCES: Thor

Heavy metal feet can crush enemies

Thor hopes his brother, Loki, will be merciful, but submits himself to the Destroyer to save the town.

MALEKITH

Dark Elf warlord

Face scarred by
Thor's lightning

Malekith is the vengeful leader of
the Dark Elves. He is so old that
the present universe is toxic to him.
Malekith waits in hibernation for
5,000 years until the Convergence,
when the Nine Realms overlap. His
plan is to release a weapon, the
Aether, and spread darkness
across the universe.

Armor protects vital organs
from poisonous radiation

Malekith and his forces make
their final stand in Greenwich,
England, the focal point of
the Convergence.

Gloves needed to
touch toxic objects

MASTER OF PATIENCE

The Aether is an ancient force
of infinite destruction that
resembles a red cloud of fluid
and gas. Odin's father, Bor, steals
the Aether and hides it from
Malekith, but the Dark Elf waits
for eons until Jane Foster
rediscovers it.

DATA FILE

AFFILIATION: Dark Elves,
Aether, Infinity Stones
KEY STRENGTHS: Strength,
durability, regeneration, long
life, Dark Elf army, Aether
APPEARANCES: Thor:
The Dark World

Boots prevent contact
with the elements

TOTAL CONTROL

Malekith draws the Aether
out of Jane Foster and
infects himself. The Aether
is an Infinity Stone that
controls reality, but its
incredible power comes
at a deadly cost.

SCRAPPER

Scavengers of Sakaar

Castaway inhabitants of the planet Sakaar are known as Scrappers. Most, but not all, are humanoid. At first, Sakaar's ruler, the Grandmaster, liked to name them, but he quickly ran out of ideas and began assigning numbers. Scrappers scrounge the garbage heaps of Sakaar for recyclables, food, and valuable goods they can sell.

Ancestral underarm hair headdress

DATA FILE

AFFILIATION: Grandmaster, Valkyrie, Sakaar
KEY STRENGTHS: Resourceful, resilient, persistent
APPEARANCES: Thor: Ragnarok

Festive clan mask

SCRAPPER STYLE

Scrappers wear colorful tribal costumes made from salvaged materials. The Grandmaster encourages flamboyant outfits and organizes a parade of the best for his own entertainment.

SORTING TIME

When Thor crash-lands on Sakaar, he is immediately captured by Scrappers. Lately, new arrivals fall into two categories: fighters who can be sold to the Grandmaster as gladiators ... and edibles.

Cobbled-together magno-rifle

VALKYRIE

Willful warrior

BOUNTY HUNTER
On the planet Sakaar, Val is known as Scrapper #142. She captures new arrivals on Sakaar, like Thor, and sells them to the Grandmaster for his Contest of Champions. The Grandmaster considers her "the best."

Dragonfang sword

Val was once a member of Asgard's elite women warriors known as the Valkyrie. When the wrathful Hela wipes them all out while trying to escape her prison, only Val survives. Val runs away to Sakaar, trying to forget her past, but Thor convinces her to return to Asgard and help him defeat Hela.

Ragged Valkyrie cape

Val dons her Valkyrie armor once more and fires a skiff cannon at Hela's wolf Fenris.

Gilded leather belt

SPORTING SPECTATOR
Seated on her ship *Warsong* hovering above the arena, Val watches the fight between Thor and Hulk. She shows interest—momentarily—when Thor looks like he might win the contest.

One of two deadly knives

Costly tracker boots

DATA FILE
AFFILIATION: The Valkyrie, Grandmaster, Asgard, Thor, Hulk
KEY STRENGTHS: Strength, long life, agility, speed, combat skills
APPEARANCES: Thor: Ragnarok

HELA

Goddess of Death

Hela is Odin's oldest child. Once the Executioner of Asgard, Hela led Odin's army in his conquest of the Nine Realms. Though Odin turned to peace, Hela's evil ambition was unstoppable. She rebelled and Odin was forced to imprison his daughter.

Headdress changes shape at will

Mantle of Darkness

Outfit magically repairs itself

CLAIMING THE THRONE

When Hela returns to Asgard she is upset that no one remembers her. Asgard's elite warriors, the Einherjar, try to stop her, but Hela single-handedly wipes out the entire army.

DATA FILE

AFFILIATION: Asgard, Hel
KEY STRENGTHS: Near invincibility, magical weapons, strength, speed
APPEARANCES: Thor: Ragnarok

Hela tried to escape prison before. She killed almost all of Asgard's Valkyrie in the attempt.

DEADLY POWERS

Hela can magically summon an unlimited number of weapons, conjuring necroswords, axes, and spikes from thin air. She has an insatiable desire for power and no remorse for the immense destruction she causes.

SKURGE

Disillusioned destroyer

Lethal ax was created by Hela

Skurge thinks tattoos make him attractive

Skurge is an Asgardian warrior who fought alongside Thor against the invading Marauders. Skurge is later assigned to guard the Bifrost bridge when Heimdall is banished from Asgard by Loki, disguised as Odin. Skurge is a born survivor, switching loyalties from Odin to Hela to save himself when she invades.

MISUNDERSTOOD

Skurge may appear to be a traitor at times, but his main motivation is just to survive. He carries out Hela's bidding because otherwise she would destroy him, but when battle breaks out, he tries to avoid hurting others.

Armor forged by Dwarves

Sigil decorated with rare blue gems

FINAL DISOBEDIENCE

Hela recruits Skurge to be her Executioner, but Skurge becomes appalled by her cruelty. When it matters most, Skurge disobeys his mistress, giving his life to save the people of Asgard.

Skurge serves as Bifrost guardian, but uses the opportunity to plunder the Nine Realms for souvenirs.

Armored boots are jointed to allow for movement

DATA FILE

AFFILIATION: Asgard, Bifrost, Hela
KEY STRENGTHS: Strength, adaptability, skilled combatant
APPEARANCES: Thor: Ragnarok

THE GRANDMASTER

Game maker

Daily changing hairstyle to suit his mood

Creative and devious mind

The Grandmaster rules over the planet Sakaar and is the creator of a deadly gladiator tournament called the Contest of Champions. He is one of the oldest beings in the universe and the brother of the powerful and mysterious Collector. He leads a luxurious and indulgent lifestyle from inside his palace tower at the city center.

Ring displays a curious gem

MASTER OF CEREMONIES

The Grandmaster's Contest of Champions pits the greatest warriors of Sakaar against each other to entertain the people. The Grandmaster promises the winner their freedom, though his latest champion, Hulk, is happy to stay.

Luxurious gold weave robe

THE CONTEST OF CHAMPIONS

The Grandmaster and Loki watch the battle between Thor and Hulk. The Grandmaster doesn't want Thor to win and gain his freedom. So he cheats and stuns Thor with his "obedience disk."

Shimmering silver loungepants

DATA FILE

AFFILIATION: Sakaar, Topaz, The Collector
KEY STRENGTHS: Long life, manipulation, charisma
APPEARANCES: Thor: Ragnarok

Blue toenail polish matches fingernails and chin stripe

With his loyal lieutenant, Topaz, ready and willing to use her lethal melt stick, the Grandmaster explains the Contest rules to Thor and Loki.

TOPAZ

Fierce fixer

MERCILESS

Topaz lacks empathy for those she considers beneath her. Topaz's dismissive nature makes her an enemy to anyone she finds irritating, especially Valkyrie.

Sakaarian facial markings

Topaz is the Grandmaster's second-in-command and chief of the Sakaarian Guard. She has many roles, including the Grandmaster's personal bodyguard, food tester, accountant, head of planetary security and the air force, and the Grandmaster's all-purpose "fixer." Topaz is nearly always at the Grandmaster's side ... except when everyone revolts against him and he is overthrown.

Custom-tailored armor

HASTY SOLUTIONS

Topaz believes in practicing tough love with Sakaar's citizens (emphasis on "tough"). She's quick to hand the Grandmaster his melt stick any time someone refuses to fall in line.

Topaz pursues Valkyrie and her friends, but her ship crashes—thanks to Bruce Banner.

DATA FILE

AFFILIATION: Grandmaster
KEY STRENGTHS: Ace pilot, nasty weapons, strength of the Sakaarian Guard
APPEARANCES: Thor: Ragnarok

KORG

Stone gladiator

A BIT CRUMBLY

Korg is a rock-like Kronan, but he is smaller than average and not quite as durable. Aware of his fragility, he just warms up the crowd before the main fight.

Body composed of perishable rock

Leather harness

Korg is a prisoner on the planet Sakaar, where he is a gladiator in the Contest of Champions. When Thor is brought in as a new gladiator, Korg befriends him. Thor later directs Valkyrie to help Korg and his gladiator friends escape. On the way out, Korg meets Loki and they head for Asgard.

WELCOMING THOR

Korg shows Thor around the gladiator stable. Korg once tried starting a revolution but failed. As punishment, he was condemned to be a gladiator.

Korg and Miek are friends. After their escape, they help fight Hela's forces on Asgard. Korg accidentally steps on Miek, but he survives.

Leather tasset protects thighs

Powerful fists

DATA FILE

AFFILIATION: Sakaar, Contest of Champions, Thor, Miek
KEY STRENGTHS: Strength, likability, skilled combatant
APPEARANCES: Thor: Ragnarok

FENRIS

Undead wolf

Hela rides a ferocious War Wolf named Fenris during her conquest of the Nine Realms. Though fallen in battle, Hela brings Fenris back from the dead using Odin's Eternal Flame. Fenris terrorizes Asgard until a struggle with the Hulk sends him falling from the brink of Asgard, just before Ragnarok begins.

DATA FILE

AFFILIATION: Hela, Asgard
KEY STRENGTHS: Strength, speed, nearly invincible, rapid healing, powerful jaws
APPEARANCES: Thor: Ragnarok

Penetrating eyes see body heat

Coarse, matted hair

Powerful, fast-moving legs

ANIMAL INTELLIGENCE

Fenris is highly intelligent. Under Hela's orders he tries to keep the Asgardians from escaping over the Rainbow Bridge. He would have succeeded, if not for Hulk.

DEADLY DOG

Fenris is a fearsome beast. His eyes glow like fire and his skin is bulletproof. His teeth are like knives—and one of the few things that manage to puncture Hulk's tough skin.

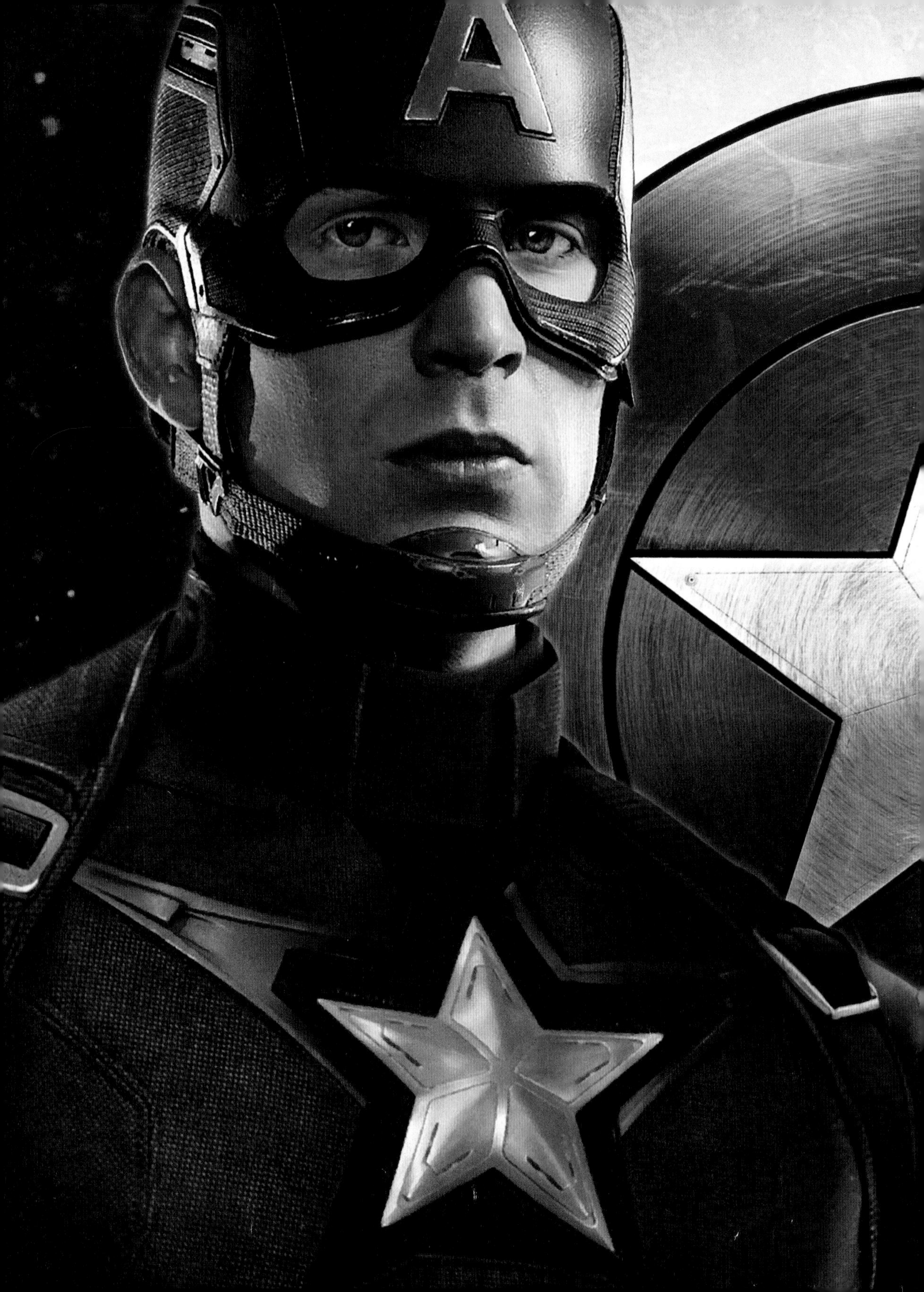

CAPTAIN AMERICA

A good man undergoes a physical transformation that changes the course of his life. Once a sickly kid from Brooklyn, Steve Rogers becomes a war hero, national symbol, enemy of oppression, and ... a key member of the Avengers.

STEVE ROGERS
Volunteer hero

Steve Rogers is a patriotic young man from Brooklyn, New York—and the future Captain America. His small size and poor health mean most people overlook him. However, Dr. Abraham Erskine sees past Rogers's appearance and finds a prime candidate for Project Rebirth, a classified program focused on enhancing human beings to create Super Soldiers.

U.S. Military
M1 helmet

HEART OF A HERO
Steve Rogers believes it is his duty to fight just like everyone else. In his heart he sees himself a soldier, but his small size hinders military enlistment.

SECOND CHANCE
Rogers is devastated when his best friend Bucky goes to war without him. Rogers gets his chance to serve when he is selected to join Project Rebirth.

For Project Rebirth, Rogers is transformed by seven microinjections of the Super-Soldier Serum, followed by a dose of Vita-Rays.

U.S. Army
wool field
shirt

Smallest
size still
too big

JAMES BUCHANAN BARNES

Best friend

James Buchanan "Bucky" Barnes is a childhood friend of Steve Rogers. Barnes joins the army during World War II, where he is captured by the evil organization Hydra. The best friends are reunited when Rogers rescues Barnes from a secret Hydra prison and weapons factory. Bucky remains by his friend's side until a tragic mission separates them for nearly 70 years.

DATA FILE

AFFILIATION: U.S. Army, Steve Rogers, Howling Commandos

KEY STRENGTHS: Loyalty, bravery, sniper skills

APPEARANCES: Captain America: The First Avenger, Captain America: The Winter Soldier

Wool naval pea coat

Pocket contains mini AJB-43 communicator

Baggy paratrooper pants pockets

HARD GOODBYE

Barnes and Rogers attend the Stark Expo the night before Bucky ships to Europe. It's the last time the friends see each other before Rogers's transformation.

COMPETITIVE EDGE

As a member of the Howling Commandos team of soldiers, Sergeant Barnes is an unequaled marksman. Little does he know, some of his abilities were enhanced by Hydra scientist Dr. Arnim Zola while Bucky was kept as a Hydra prisoner and test subject.

U.S. paratrooper boots with M1938 leggings

Barnes and his fellow Allied prisoners accompany Steve Rogers back to base after escaping from Hydra.

CAPTAIN AMERICA

Hero of World War II

Steve Rogers is transformed into a man in peak physical condition by the Super-Soldier Serum. He becomes known as the Super Hero Captain America and is ordered to act as a poster boy for the U.S. Military. In addition to his official duties, Cap leads his own team, the Howling Commandos, in a war against the evil Nazi organization, Hydra.

Form-fitting bulletproof helmet

Multi-layered flame-resistant jacket

FREEDOM'S SHIELD

Cap's vibranium shield is his primary weapon and personal symbol. The vibranium supply of Wakanda is unknown to the world during World War II, so the rare-metal shield is one of a kind.

A recently transformed Steve Rogers uses a cab door as a shield as Hydra agent Heinz Kruger fires at him.

Ribbed leather gloves for better grip

Vibranium shield designed by industrialist Howard Stark

BROTHERS IN ARMS

When his best friend Bucky Barnes is captured, Captain America suits up. He rescues Bucky and his comrades, and then forms a new team, the Howling Commandos.

Blue-dyed U.S. paratrooper pants

After defeating Hydra, Cap crashes in the Arctic and is frozen in ice. He is found nearly 70 years later.

Leather paratrooper jump boots

SENTINEL OF LIBERTY

Modern day hero

Shield attaches magnetically to forearm

Avengers "A" logo on shoulder

After defeating Hydra leader Red Skull, Captain America lies frozen in a block of ice, lost for years. He wakes up in the present day and is given charge over Nick Fury's Avengers team. Cap leads them against aliens, robots, and terrorists, but his biggest challenge might be keeping the Avengers from destroying one another.

Strap for shield rest on back

BATTLE DRESS

Captain America's suit (designed with help from S.H.I.E.L.D. agent Phil Coulson) evolves over time, becoming less showy. The patriotic design endures until Cap joins the battle to save the world from the warlord Thanos and his alien army.

Satellite communicator in pouch

POWERFUL FRIENDS

As captain of the Avengers, Steve Rogers leads Thor, Iron Man, Hawkeye, Hulk, and Black Widow. Occasionally, he clashes with Thor and Iron Man.

Pocket contains Quinjet access card

DATA FILE

AFFILIATION: U.S. Army, S.S.R., Howling Commandos, Avengers, S.H.I.E.L.D.
KEY STRENGTHS: Strength, agility, speed, endurance, leadership
APPEARANCES: Captain America: The First Avenger, The Avengers, Captain America: The Winter Soldier, Avengers: Age of Ultron, Captain America: Civil War, Avengers: Infinity War

Armored gaiters protect lower legs

Cap refuses to give up in the ceaseless war on Hydra. After the fall of S.H.I.E.L.D., he heads to Sokovia to destroy the last few Hydra bases there.

JOHANN SCHMIDT

Nazi relic hunter

Nazi S.S. commander Heinrich Himmler promotes Johann Schmidt to be the new head of a science division known as Hydra. Working from his isolated headquarters in the Swiss Alps, Schmidt searches for a powerful ancient relic called the Tesseract. He schemes to use Hydra to destroy both the Allies and Hitler.

Red discoloration around eyes

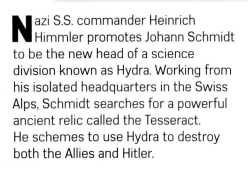

HEARTLESS

Schmidt lacks empathy and also loyalty to anything other than his own ambition. He uses Hydra to pursue greatness, but desires all the glory for himself.

Nazi S.S. science officer uniform

Leather officer's gloves

OTHERWORLDY MOTIVATION

Schmidt is obsessed with Norse mythology and supernatural objects. He isn't concerned with their mystical aspects, though. All he wants is to grasp their scientific basis in order to fully harness their power.

Luger P08 pistol concealed under uniform

Uncomfortable, itchy wool uniform

Schmidt's cruelty leads him to test his new energy weapons on fellow Nazi officers.

Nazi officer's leather boots

Impatient with Dr. Arnim Zola's cautious approach, Schmidt unleashes the full power of the Tesseract.

RED SKULL

Hydra mastermind

Nazi officer Johann Schmidt becomes horribly disfigured when he forces Dr. Erskine to inject him with an early version of the Super-Soldier Serum. The formula is otherwise effective, boosting Schmidt's physical performance and heartless ambition. He takes on the codename "Red Skull."

Face scarred by serum

An unhappy Red Skull and Arnim Zola (his second-in-command) inspect the battlefield after losing to the Howling Commandos.

DATA FILE

AFFILIATION: Hydra, Infinity Stones
KEY STRENGTHS: Intelligence, ambition, Tesseract energy weapons, Hydra's resources, Super-Soldier Serum
APPEARANCES: Captain America: The First Avenger, Avengers: Infinity War

Silver belt buckle with Hydra emblem

BAD TO WORSE
The Super-Soldier Serum amplifies characteristics already present in the recipient. For Red Skull, this includes a strong ego, determination, and a dangerous thirst for power.

Leather trench coat over Nazi uniform

DRIVING INTO BATTLE
Red Skull's custom armored car is the envy of his Nazi colleagues. The engine is powered by Tesseract energy, managed by a dashboard lined with extra gauges.

Military boots

The Tesseract beams Red Skull to the planet Vormir, where he guards the mystical Soul Stone.

PEGGY CARTER

Steadfast spy

Agent Peggy Carter serves in the British Air Force and Special Air Service before joining the Strategic Scientific Reserve (S.S.R.) in 1940. Carter oversees the training of Project Rebirth candidates at Camp Lehigh, where she meets Steve Rogers. The two fall in love, but are tragically separated for nearly 70 years.

DATA FILE

AFFILIATIONS: U.S. Military, S.S.R., Project Rebirth, S.H.I.E.L.D., Captain America
KEY STRENGTHS: Determination, wisdom, loyalty, self-sacrifice
APPEARANCES: Captain America: The First Avenger, Captain America: The Winter Soldier, Avengers: Age of Ultron, Ant-Man, Captain America: Civil War

Metal S.S.R. insignia

FEARLESS AGENT

Agent Carter doesn't wait around for orders. She chases assassin Heinz Kruger on foot after he infiltrates the S.S.R. lab.

Carter is Steve Rogers's biggest supporter. She accompanies him to the lab where he is transformed.

Two-piece wool U.S. Army dress uniform

S.H.I.E.L.D. FOUNDER

Peggy Carter's contributions are undervalued by S.S.R. management until Howard Stark asks her to help him create a secret organization known as S.H.I.E.L.D.

Carter remains a top S.H.I.E.L.D. commander for years. She oversees Hank Pym and Janet van Dyne's missions.

TIMOTHY "DUM DUM" DUGAN

Howling Commando leader

Sergeant Timothy Dugan is a founding member of the Howling Commandos team. They are led by Captain America and their objective is to defeat the secret Nazi research organization Hydra. Dugan takes command of the team following Cap's disappearance. After the war, Dum Dum works with S.H.I.E.L.D. on missions to keep America safe.

Dum Dum's signature bowler hat

Thick handlebar mustache

FIGHT FOR JUSTICE
Dum Dum is a close friend of Bucky Barnes. They are both taken prisoner by Hydra during World War II and later rescued by Captain America. Their experience in captivity motivates them to join forces and wipe out Hydra.

Hydra-upgraded Sten MkII submachine gun

BIRTH OF THE HOWLERS
After their rescue from Hydra, Dum Dum and his comrades recuperate in London. There, Captain America asks them to join his team. Dum Dum agrees, but insists that Cap first buys them a round of drinks.

Wool army pants

DATA FILE
AFFILIATION: U.S. Army, S.S.R., S.H.I.E.L.D., Captain America, Howling Commandos
KEY STRENGTHS: Commitment, honor, bravery, U.S. Army training
APPEARANCES: Captain America: The First Avenger

Dum Dum leads the Howling Commandos in their capture of Red Skull's Hydra headquarters in the Swiss Alps.

GABE JONES

Howling Commando

After graduating from university, Gabe Jones joined the U.S. Army's all-black 92nd Infantry. He is later captured and forced to build weapons for Hydra. Jones is freed when Captain America arrives to rescue another captive, Bucky Barnes. Jones subsequently joins the Howling Commandos as their heavy weapons specialist.

U.S. Infantry garrison cap

Regulation military haircut

U.S. Army uniform

STRONGER TOGETHER
Gabe Jones and Dum Dum Dugan are good friends, having served in the army together. They escape from a Hydra prison camp aboard a stolen tank.

IN THE FIELD
Gabe is a handy teammate to have behind enemy lines. He serves as the Howlers' interpreter and is also good at adapting any unusual Hydra weapons and vehicles that they manage to capture.

DATA FILE
AFFILIATION: U.S. Army, Howling Commandos
KEY STRENGTHS: Speaks German and French, army training, marksmanship
APPEARANCES: Captain America: The First Avenger

Arnimhilation 99L assault rifle

JACQUES DERNIER

Howling Commando

Jacques "Frenchie" Dernier is from Marseille, France. During World War II he was captured by the Nazis and sent to a Hydra labor camp and weapons factory. There he befriended Dum Dum Dugan and his other future Howling Commandos teammates. After their escape, he became the Howlers' explosives expert.

BOMBER
Jacques Dernier hones his bomb-making skills by sabotaging Hydra equipment while a prisoner. His antics cost him a week without food rations. He delights in blowing up Hydra tanks when he is eventually freed.

French wool cap

SELF-MADE SOLDIER
Jacques Dernier was an operative in the French Resistance. He is the only Howling Commando who was not officially a soldier in an Allied army.

Hydra-upgraded Sten MkII

DATA FILE
AFFILIATION: French Resistance, Howling Commandos, Captain America
KEY STRENGTHS: Explosives expert
APPEARANCES: Captain America: The First Avenger

JAMES MONTGOMERY FALSWORTH

Howling Commando

British paratrooper beret with Union Flag badge

Mills Bomb (hand grenade)

James Montgomery Falsworth is an expert battle strategist. He hails from Birmingham, England, and served as a Major in His Majesty's 3rd Independent Parachute Regiment. Falsworth was taken prisoner by Hydra in 1943 and forced to work in a weapons factory before escaping and joining the Howling Commandos.

HIGHLY HONORED

Falsworth is the most decorated Howler. His service medals include the Order of Burma, Africa Star, War Medal, and Defense Medal.

Sten MkII submachine gun

Following their escape from Hydra, Falsworth and friends are asked by Steve Rogers to join the Howling Commandos. Farnsworth enlists first.

Ammo belt

Pouch with three ammo clips

Wool and leather jacket

DATA FILE

AFFILIATION: Howling Commandos, Captain America
KEY STRENGTHS: Tactical mind, paratrooper, espionage, marksmanship
APPEARANCES: Captain America: The First Avenger

WAR ON HYDRA

As a member of the Howling Commandos, Falsworth helps plan a campaign to eliminate Hydra from Europe.

Cotton gaiters over leather boots

JIM MORITA

Howling Commando

Jim Morita is a Japanese American and native of Fresno, California. He served in the U.S. Army until he was captured by Hydra and forced to work in an enemy weapons factory. After escaping, he joins the Howling Commandos as their communications specialist, intercepting secret transmissions.

U.S. Army knitted wool jeep cap

U.S. Army jacket

RADIO MAN

As a communications specialist, Morita intercepts Hydra's coded messages, allowing him to locate Nazi scientist Arnim Zola aboard a train. Morita also facilitates Steve Rogers's last call to Peggy Carter before Rogers crashes in Antarctica.

THE LONG HAUL

Morita and the Howlers' campaign to rid Europe of Hydra continues through a cold winter in the Alps until they capture Red Skull's secret base.

Hydra Zolanator 2000X assault rifle

DATA FILE

AFFILIATION: Howling Commandos, Captain America, U.S. Army
KEY STRENGTHS: Radio and telecommunications expertise, tech enthusiast, marksmanship
APPEARANCES: Captain America: The First Avenger

DR. ARNIM ZOLA

Engineering genius

Hydra's top scientist is Dr. Arnim Zola, the second-in-command to Johann Schmidt (a.k.a. Red Skull). Zola develops high-tech weapons and other advanced technology for Hydra. Zola wasn't always a fanatic, but his devotion grew under the leadership of Red Skull. Nonetheless, Zola betrays his commander to save himself.

Fedora from stylish Berlin boutique

Zola's scientific mind makes him a top S.H.I.E.L.D. recruit. However, he uses his position to rebuild Hydra.

Bow tie has become a signature look

Hydra pin

SEEKER OF POWER
Zola harnesses the limitless energy of the Tesseract (itself powered by an Infinity Stone) to build weapons for Hydra.

THOUGHT CONTROL
Before dying, Zola's mind is transferred to a mainframe computer. In this state he develops an algorithm used by Hydra to eliminate threats.

DATA FILE
AFFILIATION: Hydra, S.H.I.E.L.D.
KEY STRENGTHS: Scientific genius, strong survival instinct
APPEARANCES: Captain America: The First Avenger, Captain America: The Winter Soldier

HEINZ KRUGER

Hydra assassin

German native Heinz Kruger is a devoted Hydra agent sent to recover the Super-Soldier Serum from the Strategic Scientific Reserve (S.S.R.) lab, and eliminate the defector, Dr. Erskine. He infiltrates Project Rebirth using the identity of State Department agent Fred Clemson. Once caught, Kruger commits suicide by cyanide capsule.

Fanatical mind brainwashed by Hydra

Cyanide capsule hidden in tooth

Walther P38 pistol

M1928 Thompson submachine gun

MAN WITH A PLAN

Kruger detonates a bomb on the balcony of the S.S.R. lab, just before stealing the Super-Soldier Serum, shooting Dr. Erskine, and fleeing to his car.

Kruger attempts to escape in the *Fieser Dorsch* mini submarine.

HARD TO STOP

As he flees the S.S.R. lab, Kruger is nearly shot by Agent Carter. The assassin continues, determined to make his escape, until Steve Rogers pulls him from his departing submarine.

DATA FILE

AFFILIATION: Hydra

KEY STRENGTHS: Hydra training, espionage, fanaticism

APPEARANCES: Captain America: The First Avenger

DR. ABRAHAM ERSKINE

Super-Soldier creator

A talented German scientist, Dr. Abraham Erskine got Hitler's attention by developing a Super-Soldier Serum. Nazi officer Johann Schmidt captures Erskine and forces the scientist to inject him with the untested formula. When Erskine escapes, he joins the U.S. Strategic Scientific Reserve (S.S.R.) and their Project Rebirth.

Felt Fedora hat

Prescription glasses

APPROVAL

Impressed with Steve Rogers's five attempts to enlist, Erskine approves Rogers's U.S. Military application.

Concerned for Rogers, Erskine tells Howard Stark to stop the experiment, but Rogers wants to continue.

Custom three-piece suit

FINDING A HERO

Erskine's Super-Soldier formula amplifies the personality of the recipient. Therefore Erskine selects a good man to be the test subject: Steve Rogers.

68

HOWARD STARK

Inventor and businessman

MANY TALENTS

Howard Stark is an engineer, inventor, entrepreneur, risk-taker, and astute businessman. His confident personality rubs some people the wrong way, including his son, Tony, although Tony learns to appreciate his father later in life.

Slick haircut

Fancy suit to impress investors

Howard Stark is the father of Tony Stark. During World War II, he is a member of the Strategic Scientific Reserve (S.S.R.) and develops equipment for Captain America and his Howling Commandos. Following the war, Stark founds S.H.I.E.L.D. with Peggy Carter. He later angers Hank Pym by trying to duplicate Ant-Man technology.

REVERSE ENGINEERING

Hydra creates advanced technology by studying the mystical object known as the Tesseract. Stark examines captured Hydra hardware to make something even better for Allied forces.

Howard Stark builds and maintains all the technology in the S.S.R. labs. He takes charge of the controls during Steve Rogers's transformation.

There were other more complex designs to choose from, but Captain America chooses a round vibranium shield created by Howard Stark.

DATA FILE

AFFILIATION: S.S.R., S.H.I.E.L.D., Stark Industries
KEY STRENGTHS: Ambition, scientific genius, creativity, wealth
APPEARANCES: Iron Man 2, Captain America: The First Avenger, Ant-Man, Captain America: Civil War

WINTER SOLDIER

Bionic-armed soldier

After falling off a train during World War II, Bucky Barnes is captured by Hydra and experimented on by Dr. Arnim Zola. His brain is reprogrammed to transform him into a secret weapon: the Winter Solider. He hibernates between missions to delay aging, awakening with orders to destroy Nick Fury and Captain America.

Black grease reduces glare and hides identity

Red Soviet Communist Star on metal arm

ERASING THE PAST

Bucky's memories return in fragments. He recalls falling, Zola replacing his arm, and his early training. He also remembers Steve Rogers. In response, Hydra leader Alexander Pierce orders his scientists to wipe Bucky's mind again.

Ammo belt

DATA FILE

AFFILIATION: Hydra, Avengers, Captain America
KEY STRENGTHS: Strength, speed, agility, endurance, cybernetic arm
APPEARANCES: Captain America: The Winter Soldier, Ant-Man, Captain America: Civil War, Avengers: Infinity War

Soviet 1975 pilot glove

Soviet special ops pants

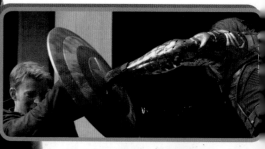

The Winter Soldier fights Captain America in the city streets, which is when he recognizes his old friend.

ALMOST FLAWLESS

The Winter Soldier is a master assassin thanks to both Hydra and Soviet training. As long as his programming is active, he is a remorseless killer; he is even responsible for the deaths of Tony Stark's parents. His only "weaknesses" are his memories of his past and the good man that he really is.

Old Russian army boots

JAMES BUCHANAN BARNES

Bionic-armed hero

Steve Rogers's efforts to reach his brainwashed best friend eventually triggers Bucky's memories. Bucky goes on the run, trying to remember his past. Meanwhile, the terrorist Helmut Zemo frames Bucky for the Sokovia Accords bombing, placing Bucky at the heart of the Avengers' Civil War. He finds sanctuary in Wakanda.

Long, untidy hair

After Bucky's recovery, King T'Challa calls him back into military service when Thanos invades.

Red star is now absent

Wakandan vibranium arm

BATTLE OF HEROES

When the Avengers face an internal battle, Bucky stands alongside his longtime ally, Steve Rogers. They face off against Tony Stark at the Leipzig-Halle Airport.

M249 Paratrooper SAW assault rifle

WHITE WOLF

In the African country of Wakanda, Bucky is known as the White Wolf. King T'Challa no longer holds a grudge against Bucky for the death of his father, after he learns the villain Helmut Zemo is really responsible.

Bucky and Rocket make a good team during the Battle of Wakanda. Rocket envies Bucky's high-powered weapon, though.

Black cargo pants

FALCON

High-flying hero

After retiring from military service, former U.S. Air Force pararescue officer Samuel Thomas Wilson finds work at Veterans Affairs. He befriends Steve Rogers and helps him and Natasha Romanoff fight the Hydra uprising. He joins the Avengers and fights against Thanos's invasion of Wakanda.

Smart goggles linked to Redwing

Bulletproof chest armor

DATA FILE

AFFILIATION: U.S. Air Force, Avengers, Captain America
KEY STRENGTHS: Air Force training, flight, shields (via wings), Redwing drone
APPEARANCES: Captain America: The Winter Soldier, Avengers: Age of Ultron, Ant-Man, Captain America: Civil War, Avengers: Infinity War

Flexible body armor plating

Gauntlet with Redwing touch-pad controls

FLIGHT AND FIGHT

Falcon's exosuit is fitted with integrated miniature jet engines, which power his flight. The wings can be used as weapons.

Jointed mechanical arm brace

Redwing launches on voice command and features retractable wings, twin machine guns, and remote scanning cameras.

WINGED WARRIOR

Sam Wilson's EXO-7 Falcon jetpack allows him to fly. On his backpack is Redwing, a small, maneuverable drone built by Stark Industries.

Reinforced kneepads for rough touchdowns

Nylon reinforced Mylar vanes

Shock-absorbing landing boots

SHARON CARTER

Codename: Agent 13

STRONG WILLED

Carter has a habit of going against her superiors—both at S.H.I.E.L.D. and the CIA. This isolates her and creates enemies. Fortunately, she has a knack for always choosing the right side.

Inspired to follow in the footsteps of her great-aunt, Peggy Carter, Sharon Carter joins S.H.I.E.L.D. Nick Fury assigns her to watch over Steve Rogers just before Fury's attempted assassination. After the fall of S.H.I.E.L.D., Carter is recruited by the CIA. She works with Everett Ross at the Joint Counter Terrorism Center in Berlin.

When Carter speaks at her aunt Peggy's funeral, Steve Rogers learns the two are related.

Tactical vest for field work

ALLY AT S.H.I.E.L.D. HQ

Sharon Carter is one of the good agents still working at S.H.I.E.L.D. during Hydra's uprising. She supports Steve Rogers, Natasha Romanoff, and Nick Fury.

Sharon and Steve Rogers bond after Peggy's funeral. She helps him find and protect Bucky Barnes on the run.

Flexible stretch pants for active duty

Versatile ankle boots

DATA FILE

AFFILIATION: S.H.I.E.L.D., CIA, Steve Rogers, Joint Counter Terrorism Center, Everett Ross

KEY STRENGTHS: S.H.I.E.L.D. and CIA training, espionage, determination

APPEARANCES: Captain America: The Winter Soldier, Captain America: Civil War

JASPER SITWELL

Hydra double-agent

Jasper Sitwell is a long-serving S.H.I.E.L.D. agent with a wealth of experience. Agent Phil Coulson assigns Sitwell to cover up the New Mexico incident involving Thor and his hammer. Sitwell is also charged with locating Loki prior to the Chitauri invasion. However, Sitwell is later proven to be a secret Hydra agent.

DATA FILE

AFFILIATION: S.H.I.E.L.D., Hydra
KEY STRENGTHS: Hydra and S.H.I.E.L.D. training, high security clearance
APPEARANCES: Thor, The Avengers, Captain America: The Winter Soldier

Smart and devious mind

S.H.I.E.L.D. lapel pin amuses other Hydra loyalists

TAKING THE LEAD

Sitwell takes over when Steve Rogers disobeys orders from his superiors. Sitwell orders Brock Rumlow and his S.T.R.I.K.E. team to hunt Rogers down.

Sitwell is an office worker. He orders others into danger while he remains safe.

UNDER VALUED

Like most Hydra agents, Sitwell thinks he is a good guy. Nonetheless, his boss, Alexander Pierce, believes Sitwell is a liability to their cause and sends the Winter Soldier to eliminate him.

GEORGES BATROC

Hostage taker

Batroc monitors S.H.I.E.L.D. communications. When there is radio silence he knows something is amiss.

Georges Batroc is a highly-skilled mercenary hired to hijack S.H.I.E.L.D.'s ship, *Lemurian Star*. Batroc takes the ship and holds its passengers hostage, but his mission is cut short when Agent Brock Rumlow, Captain America, and Black Widow retake the ship. Batroc escapes, but is caught later.

Harness carrying tactical gear

Throwing knife

Favorite purple and gold shirt

Major Mel paramilitary boots

MAN TO MAN

Captain America chases Batroc onto the deck of the ship, where they fight. Batroc suggests Cap is hiding behind his shield, so Cap places it on his back.

DATA FILE

AFFILIATION: Mercenary
KEY STRENGTHS: Mixed martial arts expert (especially savate), munitions expert, espionage, military tactics
APPEARANCES: Captain America: The Winter Soldier

A SERIOUS MAN

Batroc is a former member of the French Foreign Legion and French Intelligence (DGSE). He is wanted by Interpol for violent crimes.

BROCK RUMLOW

S.H.I.E.L.D. traitor

S.H.I.E.L.D. agent Brock Rumlow is a Black Ops S.T.R.I.K.E. team commander who partners with Captain America and Black Widow. He is an ambitious agent, with top hand-to-hand combat skills. Secretly working for Hydra, Rumlow is ordered to assassinate Captain America.

Special Ops
tactical uniform

TRAINED KILLER

Brock Rumlow is an expert marksman who is skilled with a wide range of weapons. Using rifles, pistols, knives, and grenade launchers, he works as a covert assassin against pirates and terrorists.

Bulletproof
vest underneath

Pistol holster

S.T.R.I.K.E.
paratrooper pants

TOP S.H.I.E.L.D. AGENT

Rumlow leads a S.T.R.I.K.E. team, including Captain America and Black Widow, to recapture the ship *Lemurian Star* from pirates and free the prisoners.

Throwing knife

Steyr AUG A3 with
a DCL-110 sight

S.H.I.E.L.D.
combat boots

Rumlow is just following orders when he turns against his teammate, Captain America. It isn't personal ... yet.

CROSSBONES

Mercenary with a grudge

Brock Rumlow suffers severe burns and nerve damage during the Hydra uprising. With both Hydra and S.H.I.E.L.D. now underground, Rumlow adopts the codename Crossbones and works as a mercenary and terrorist. He is motivated by getting revenge against Captain America for ruining his life.

Mask hides terrible scarring

"Crossbones" armored chest plate

Bulletproof body armor

FULLY LOADED

Crossbones arrives with a vehicle-mounted MK19 grenade launcher and other military-grade munitions to steal a deadly biological weapon from a CDC facility in Lagos, Nigeria.

FORCE-MULTIPLIER

Crossbones wears a pair of force-multiplier gauntlets that punch his opponents with enough power to send them flying. When their blades are extended, an impact means certain death.

Surplus ammunition and gauntlet attachments

Mechanical gauntlets

DATA FILE

AFFILIATION: S.H.I.E.L.D., Hydra
KEY STRENGTHS: S.H.I.E.L.D. and Hydra training. Crossbones: immune to pain and stuns, force-multiplier gauntlets
APPEARANCES: Captain America: The Winter Soldier, Captain America: Civil War

Separate knee armor allows flexibility

Crossbones triggers a bomb hidden in his suit in the hope of destroying Captain America in the explosion.

Fireproof biohazard boots

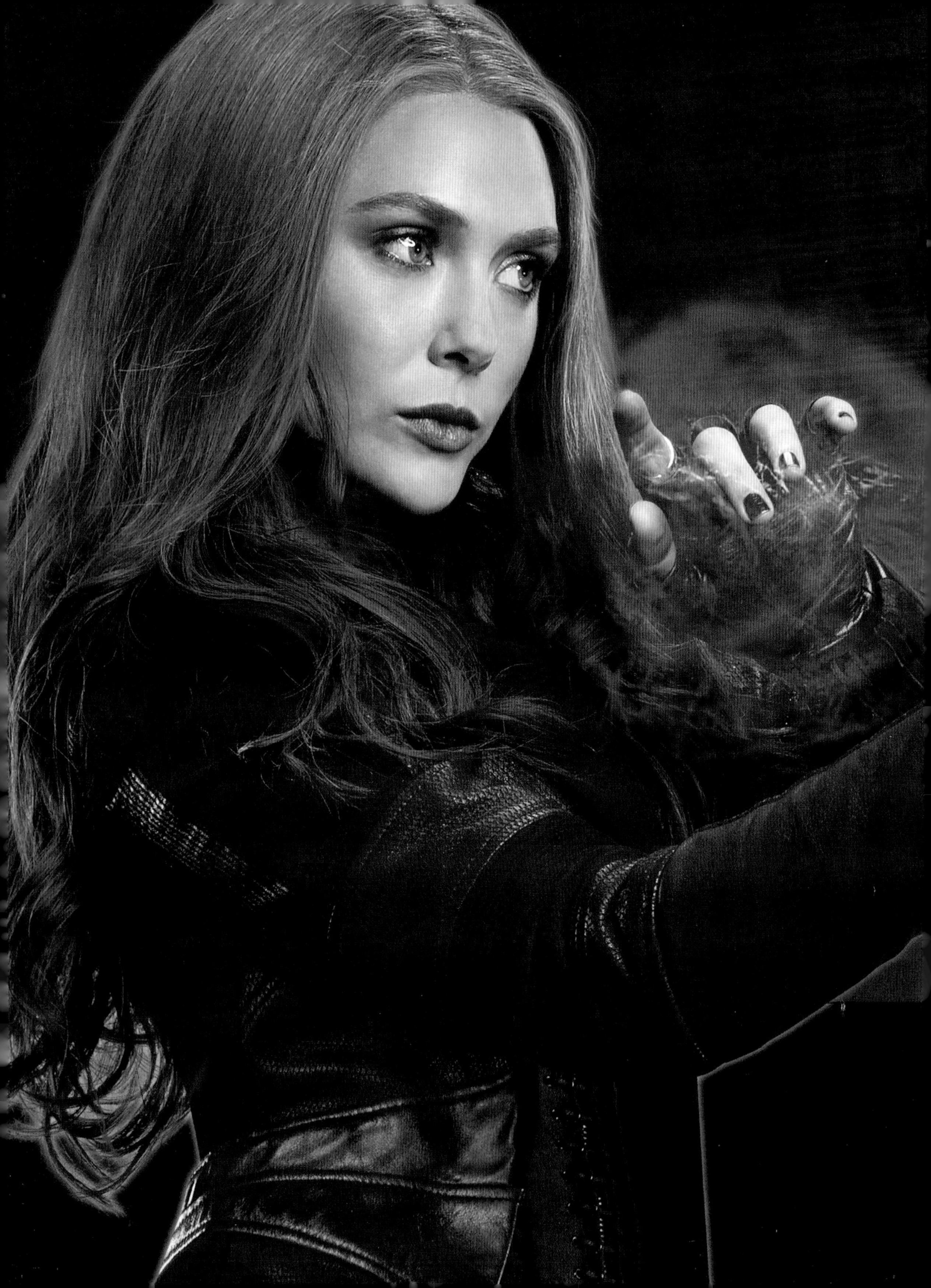

THE AVENGERS

The Avengers are a team with unusual talents, formed by S.H.I.E.L.D.'s Nick Fury to protect the world from extraterrestrial threats. They face terrorists, androids, and alien armies, leading to a war over the precious and powerful Infinity Stones.

NICK FURY

Director of S.H.I.E.L.D.

Colonel Nicholas "Nick" Joseph Fury is the gruff, no-nonsense director of S.H.I.E.L.D. and founder of the Avengers Initiative. He fakes his own death to survive during the rise of Hydra, but remains available to help when Ultron threatens Earth. Fury also calls in Captain Marvel when Thanos wields the Infinity Stones.

Eye patch conceals blind eye

Bulletproof 9-ply Kevlar vest

Nick Fury is the first to brief Steve Rogers when he awakes.

Smith & Wesson M&P sidearm

TAKING THE LEAD

Nick Fury has a hands-on command style. He doesn't lead from an office. He prefers to be at a S.H.I.E.L.D. Helicarrier helm and interact with agents directly.

PROVIDING BACKUP

After S.H.I.E.L.D.'s collapse, Fury works from the shadows. Maria Hill keeps an eye on the Avengers, allowing Fury to step in when needed, such as when he helps evacuate civilians in Sokovia.

Knife hidden in boot

S.H.I.E.L.D.-issue boots contain security microchips

DATA FILE

AFFILIATION: S.H.I.E.L.D., Avengers
KEY STRENGTHS: Survivor, leadership, CIA training, command of S.H.I.E.L.D. resources
APPEARANCES: Iron Man, Iron Man 2, Captain America: The First Avenger, The Avengers, Captain America: The Winter Soldier, Avengers: Age of Ultron, Avengers: Infinity War, Captain Marvel

MARIA HILL

S.H.I.E.L.D. Deputy Director

Stark Industries
encrypted earpiece

Fire-resistant
S.H.I.E.L.D.
jumpsuit

Agent Maria Hill is the Deputy Director of S.H.I.E.L.D. She works closely with Director Nick Fury. While they don't always see eye to eye, Hill's forthright feedback is intended to provide Fury with credible alternatives. When Hydra takes over S.H.I.E.L.D. and Fury is forced to fake his own death, Hill is the only person he completely trusts.

TACTICAL SPECIALIST

Like her boss, Hill works confidently from the command center of a S.H.I.E.L.D. Helicarrier. She provides vital support during the Battle of New York and the Ultron Offensive in Sokovia.

FURY'S RIGHT HAND

After the collapse of S.H.I.E.L.D., Maria Hill serves as Nick Fury's eyes and ears. She is a secret channel of communication for him to the Avengers and other covert agents embedded in the field.

Glock 19 sidearm in
adjustable holster

Site of healed
mission injury

DATA FILE

AFFILIATION: S.H.I.E.L.D., Avengers, Stark Industries, Nick Fury

KEY STRENGTHS: Determination, leadership, S.H.I.E.L.D. training

APPEARANCES: The Avengers, Captain America: The Winter Soldier, Avengers: Age of Ultron, Avengers: Infinity War, Captain Marvel

Compact weapon
concealed in boot

Hill continues to work with the Avengers as an employee of Stark Industries, providing mission critical support.

DR. BRUCE BANNER
Radiation expert

Mild-mannered scientist Bruce Banner participates in a military program attempting to recreate the Super-Soldier Serum that created Captain America. A lab accident transforms him into the Hulk—a beast controlled by pure rage. Banner's expertise with gamma radiation proves useful to the Avengers, as does his powerful alter-ego.

Shaggy hair

SUPER TEAM
Banner and Tony Stark make a great research team, combining their skills in technology, science, and innovation.

Crossed arms suggest shyness

Thrift store jacket

Stark's Hulkbuster suit is created specifically to subdue the Hulk. When Banner dons it for the Battle of Wakanda, however, it proves no match against Thanos.

IN CONTROL?
Bruce Banner and Hulk constantly fight for control of their shared body. Banner worries he is losing the battle, especially after spending several years as the Hulk on the planet Sakaar.

Transforming into the Hulk is a painful process. Banner hates that he loses control.

HULK

Man and monster

The Hulk is Bruce Banner's monstrous alter-ego. After getting dosed with gamma rays, Banner now transforms into the Hulk any time he gets angry, anxious, or hurt. The Hulk is a valuable member of the Avengers, but he and Banner have a love-hate relationship, wrestling for control of their shared body.

Fist can punch holes in brick walls

ANGER AT ALIENS

Acting with newfound self-control, the Hulk helps the Avengers battle the Chitauri aliens that have invaded New York.

MASTERING HIS POWERS

After his early transformations, Hulk's unrelenting power and rage prove too much for the Avengers and they fear awakening Banner's alter-ego. However, over time, the Avengers learn to use Hulk's powers to their advantage.

After Hulk is defeated by Thanos, he changes back into Banner and refuses to transform again.

Legs able to jump hundreds of feet

Feet can stomp cars flat

On the planet Sakaar, Hulk ends up the reigning gladiator in a competition known as the Contest of Champions.

BLACK WIDOW

Super spy assassin

KGB agent Natalia Allanovna "Natasha" Romanoff was once a top Soviet assassin. S.H.I.E.L.D. agent Clint Barton was ordered to eliminate her, but he saw her potential and recruited her instead. She uses her spy skills for S.H.I.E.L.D., infiltrating Stark Industries, teaming up with Captain America, and battling alongside fellow Avengers.

Retractable electroshock wand

Widow's Bite gauntlet

A LONELY LOVE

Natasha bonds with fellow Avenger Bruce Banner over their mutual isolation from society. Their connection allows her to calm a raging Hulk, but when he disappears onboard a Quinjet, she is alone once more.

Trademark wavy red hair

Black Widow hourglass symbol

Black Widow always adapts to changing situations. In Scotland, she uses Proxima Midnight's own weapon against her.

WIDOW'S BITE

Black Widow wears an electroshock "Widow's Bite" gauntlet on each wrist. They can incapacitate opponents on contact, or fire stun projectiles.

Flexible knee armor

Titanium-plated boots

Romanoff has a long relationship with Tony Stark, from undercover assistant to the Sokovia Accords.

DATA FILE

AFFILIATION: S.H.I.E.L.D., Avengers, Tony Stark

KEY STRENGTHS: Red Room assassin training, martial arts, agility, spy skills, Widow's Bite gauntlets, electroshock batons

APPEARANCES: Iron Man 2, The Avengers, Captain America: The Winter Soldier, Avengers: Age of Ultron, Captain America: Civil War, Avengers: Infinity War

HAWKEYE

Avenging archer

The focused yet good-humored S.H.I.E.L.D. agent Clint Francis Barton (codename: Hawkeye) is an expert bowman armed with a whole arsenal of trick arrows. He becomes a founding member of the Avengers during an alien invasion masterminded by Loki. Barton tries to retire to be with his family, but is later drawn into the Avengers' Civil War.

Collapsible recurve bow

Arrow rest

A LONG HISTORY

Barton and Natasha Romanoff have a close relationship. When Romanoff was a Soviet agent, S.H.I.E.L.D. ordered Barton to eliminate her. However, seeing Natasha's potential, he recruited her instead.

DATA FILE

AFFILIATION: S.H.I.E.L.D., Avengers, Loki, Captain America
KEY STRENGTHS: Expert bowman with trick arrows, S.H.I.E.L.D. training, acrobatic abilities
APPEARANCES: Thor, The Avengers, Avengers: Age of Ultron, Captain America: Civil War

Family photo tucked inside tunic

Dressed for cold Sokovian weather

MASTER ARCHER

Hawkeye is a left-handed bowman. His custom bow features remote controls for a mechanized quiver, which prepares trick arrowheads. Hawkeye's arrowheads feature rappelling lines, EMPs, flash arrowheads, timed explosives, and impact triggers.

Bent knees help Hawkeye pull bowstring further

Straps for optional weapons holsters

During the Battle of New York, Hawkeye perches near Stark Tower, hitting invading Chitauri chariots with explosive arrows.

THANOS
Ruthless warlord

Thanos is a powerful Titan warlord obsessed with eliminating half the universe's population. He believes this will create balance by stabilizing resources and thus sustain all remaining life. With the help of his "children," Thanos raises an army and acquires the powerful Infinity Stones, granting him absolute power to realize his diabolical purpose.

Thanos has impressive strength. He easily defeats and humiliates Hulk aboard Thor's captured ship.

Infinity Gauntlet with all six stones

Closed fist activates gauntlet

BETRAYAL

Thanos has a complex relationship with his adopted daughter Gamora, whom he kidnapped as a child. She tries to eliminate him on the Knowhere Space Station before he acquires all the stones.

THE INFINITY GAUNTLET

Thanos forces the Dwarf King, Eitri, to forge a gauntlet that can harness the power of the Infinity Stones. The six stones control space, time, power, minds, souls, and reality. One by one, the Mad Titan takes them all.

DATA FILE

AFFILIATION: Chitauri army, Ronan the Accuser

KEY STRENGTHS: Strength, stamina, the Infinity Gauntlet, Chitauri army

APPEARANCES: The Avengers, Guardians of the Galaxy, Avengers: Age of Ultron, Avengers: Infinity War

Thanos acquires the last Infinity Stone from Vision's forehead, which enables him to extinguish half the universe.

CHITAURI
Alien invaders

The Chitauri are a race of cyborg aliens that serve in Thanos's army. He uses them to devastate planets like Zen-Whoberi, Gamora's homeworld. Thanos lends the Chitauri to Loki for his own conquest of Earth, but the invasion fails. As a result, the aliens' advanced weapons fall into the hands of human criminals and terrorists.

MANHATTAN MAYHEM
Once they reach New York, Chitauri forces detach from their massive Leviathans and begin their assault on the city. Pilots on flying chariots battle the Avengers in the skies.

Metal-fused skull plate

A FATAL FLAW
The Chitauri are seemingly endless in number, but they have one major weakness. Their hive mind requires connection to a mother ship. The Chitauri are stranded and perish when the Avengers destroy their ship and close their wormhole.

Breathing apparatus

Metallic exoskeleton

Energy cannon

Double thumbs

The Chitauri army arrives on Earth through a wormhole opened by Dr. Selvig using a relic known as the Tesseract.

SCARLET WITCH
Mystical sorceress

Wanda Maximoff and her brother, Pietro, gain their extraordinary powers after volunteering as subjects for Hydra experiments, which use the mystical Infinity Stone from Loki's scepter. Although she starts out as the Avengers' foe, Wanda officially becomes part of the team following the defeat of Ultron.

Mind powers include telepathy

Arms raised to project powers

Orbs of telekinetic energy

SHOCKING REALIZATION
At first, Wanda is unable to sense Ultron's mechanical mind. But when the android downloads himself into a "synthezoid" body, Wanda can suddenly read his evil intentions.

Red leather jacket

Wanda battles Thanos's forces in Wakanda as long as she can, but she and fellow Avenger Vision lose the fight.

DATA FILE
AFFILIATION: Hydra, Ultron, Avengers, Captain America, Vision, Quicksilver
KEY STRENGTHS: Telekinetic energy projection, levitation, mind control, telepathy
APPEARANCES: Captain America: The Winter Soldier, Avengers: Age of Ultron, Captain America: Civil War, Avengers: Infinity War

Sokovian high-heeled leather boots

BEWITCHING
Wanda gained a huge array of powers after undergoing the Hydra experiments. She can project psionic energy as a weapon, move objects with her mind, read people's thoughts and feelings, and even control the minds of others.

QUICKSILVER

Pietro Maximoff

Pietro Maximoff and his sister, Wanda, were orphaned when a bomb made by Stark Industries destroyed their Sokovian home. As adults they volunteered for a Hydra experiment that granted them extraordinary powers. Pietro's power is immense speed, which earns him the codename Quicksilver when he joins the Avengers.

Pietro and his sister are very close. They helped each other survive growing up on the street.

BECOMING A HERO

After Pietro and Wanda discover that Ultron intends to wipe out humanity, Pietro's desire for revenge against Tony Stark shifts to saving civilians caught in the conflict.

COMPETITIVE

Pietro and the Avenger Hawkeye develop a personal rivalry. Both are known for their quick reflexes—though Pietro outperforms. The rivalry becomes a blessing when Pietro sacrifices himself to save Hawkeye.

Special material dampens electrical charges

Gloves keep sleeves from flying up

DATA FILE

AFFILIATION: Hydra, Ultron, Avengers, Wanda Maximoff
KEY STRENGTHS: Moves at incredible speed
APPEARANCES: Captain America: The Winter Soldier, Avengers: Age of Ultron

Runner's pants

BARON STRUCKER

Hydra commander

Wolfgang Von Strucker was a top scientist working for S.H.I.E.L.D., but he was also a Hydra double-agent. When S.H.I.E.L.D. collapses, Strucker relocates to his castle in Sokovia. There he conducts research using Chitauri alien technology recovered from the Battle of New York. Once defeated, he is held in a NATO prison.

Augmented reality monocle

Concerned look as Hydra falters

Strucker and fellow Hydra scientist Dr. List are testing Chitauri technology on human subjects.

FINAL BATTLE

Strucker makes his stand against the Avengers from inside his Sokovian castle, trying to protect his secret research. He is captured by Captain America, but Ultron later brings him to an early, decisive end.

MAD SCIENTISTS

Hidden in his castle, Strucker and his lieutenant, Dr. List, experiment on Sokovian volunteers using Loki's mind-altering scepter. Only the Maximoff twins survive. Strucker and List also alter Hydra soldiers, implanting Chitauri cybernetics.

Inconspicuous jacket

Stance suggests contemplation

DATA FILE

AFFILIATION: Hydra, S.H.I.E.L.D.
KEY STRENGTHS: Scientific mind, Hydra resources
APPEARANCES: Captain America: The Winter Soldier, Avengers: Age of Ultron

ULTRON

Evil android

Ultron was created to be a peacekeeping system—an artificial intelligence meant to run Tony Stark's Iron Legion of drones and protect Earth from alien invasions. Instead, a self-righteous digital maniac was born, with an obsession to destroy the Avengers and wipe out all of mankind using a doomsday device built in Sokovia.

Leviathan anti-gravity device in palms

Red reactor glow visible through arm

DATA FILE

AFFILIATION: Tony Stark, Wanda and Pietro Maximoff, Vision

KEY STRENGTHS: Strength, durability, flight, repulsor blasts, downloadable mind, vast database of knowledge

APPEARANCES: Avengers: Age of Ultron

ENDLESS UPGRADES

After achieving consciousness, Ultron downloads himself into a damaged Iron Legion drone. He transfers from that body into a Chitauri android in Sokovia. He continuously upgrades himself from there, eventually with a strong vibranium frame.

Coolant systems and power relays

Exoskeleton incorporates vibranium from Ulysses Klaue

MAKING A MIND

Tony Stark and Bruce Banner try to create an artificial intelligence using the blueprints for a consciousness they discover in the Mind Stone from Loki's scepter.

Hydra-inspired exosuit knee mechanics

Ultron's weaponry is a combination of Tony Stark's inventions and Hydra research into alien technology.

VISION

Android Avenger

A synthetic life-form, Vision was created by Ultron using artificial human cells infused with vibranium. An Infinity Stone in his forehead instills consciousness and supernatural power. Intended as a replacement body for Ultron, the Avengers intervene and awaken someone entirely different: Vision is physically flawless and morally good.

Mind Stone mounted in forehead

Ultron designed a physically perfect body

THE PRIZE ABOVE HIS EYES

The Infinity Stone in Vision's forehead makes him a powerful addition to the Avengers. It also makes him a target for Thanos, who needs the Stone to complete his Infinity Gauntlet.

A LOVER AND A FIGHTER

Vision and Wanda Maximoff fall in love during the conflict over the Sokovia Accords. After the Avengers' Civil War, they run away to Scotland together—but, tragically, Thanos intervenes.

Gauntlets amplify control of computers and electronics

Costumes and body appearance can change at will

Cape is inspired by Thor's own

Vision is tasked with keeping Wanda at the Avengers' facility. Their relationship is tested when she tries to leave.

DATA FILE

AFFILIATION: Avengers, Tony Stark, Infinity Stones, Wanda Maximoff
KEY STRENGTHS: Flight, energy beam (via Mind Stone), strength, intelligence, phase-shifting
APPEARANCES: Avengers: Age of Ultron, Captain America: Civil War, Avengers: Infinity War

DR. HELEN CHO

Leading geneticist

Tony Stark's South Korean associate Dr. Helen Cho is a cutting-edge geneticist and inventor of the Regeneration Cradle. The device creates synthetic human tissue designed to bond seamlessly with the body. Ultron sees the immediate value in her technology, but his meddling unintentionally results in the creation of a powerful new Avenger, Vision.

Brilliant and creative mind

CRADLE OF LIFE
Dr. Cho's Regeneration Cradle is designed to heal serious injuries. Ultron shows her how to modify it to create an entire synthetic body—resulting in Vision's birth.

Lab outfit with anti-bacterial coating

COLLABORATIVE COLLEAGUE
Dr. Cho is a friend of all the Avengers and works closely with Bruce Banner and Tony Stark. When Hawkeye is seriously injured during a mission against Hydra, she helps by quickly healing him.

Ultron uses Loki's scepter to control Cho's mind, forcing her to build him a brand new body.

DATA FILE
AFFILIATION: Avengers, U-Gin Genetics, Tony Stark
KEY STRENGTHS: Ingenious scientific mind, medical expertise
APPEARANCES: Avengers: Age of Ultron

THADDEUS E. ROSS

Secretary of State

Serving as Lieutenant General in the U.S. Army, "Thunderbolt" Ross oversees a new Super-Soldier Serum program. His daughter, Elizabeth, and Bruce Banner are recruited, but when Banner transforms into the Hulk, Ross is bent on catching him. Ross is later appointed U.S. Secretary of State and tries to regulate the activities of the Avengers.

Hair colored to look younger

SOKOVIA ACCORDS
Ross enforces the Sokovia Accords, the government-controlled regulation of super-powered individuals. This brings him into conflict with the Avengers, who are not all in favor of the Accords.

Army uniform and medals traded for suit

IN CHARGE
Ross is an authoritarian. He doesn't like being disobeyed. When Captain America and his partners refuse to sign the Sokovia Accords, Ross designates them as criminal fugitives.

In his obsession to stop the Hulk, Ross plans to inject a sample of the Super-Soldier Serum into Emil Blonsky, a soldier helping him to track down Hulk.

DATA FILE
AFFILIATION: U.S. Army, U.S. State Department, Strategic Operations Command Center, Sokovia Accords
KEY STRENGTHS: Command of U.S. Military and government resources
APPEARANCES: The Incredible Hulk, Captain America: Civil War, Avengers: Infinity War

EITRI

Dwarf King

Eitri is the King of the Dwarves of Nidavellir. Their name is deceptive, for Dwarves are quite large! Eitri is entrusted by Odin with creating the magical weapons of Asgard, including Thor's hammer, Mjolnir. After Mjolnir is destroyed, Eitri helps Thor create a new hammer called Stormbreaker, believed capable of destroying Thanos.

Hair and beard are untrimmed

DATA FILE

AFFILIATION: Dwarves of Nidavellir, Thor, Asgard

KEY STRENGTHS: Can create the universe's most powerful weapons

APPEARANCES: Avengers: Infinity War

Sturdy harness strap

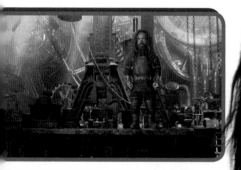

SEARCH FOR THE MASTER

Eitri's reputation as a master weapons forger is known across the universe. After his hammer is destroyed, Thor seeks Eitri out, although the Dwarf does not recognize Thor at first.

Fireproof clothing

SAD END

Thanos forces Eitri to craft the Infinity Gauntlet for him. When finished, Thanos wipes out all Eitri's people and encases Eitri's hands in metal to prevent him from crafting any more weapons.

When Thanos leaves Nidavellir, it is desolate. The forge is off and the dying star is dark.

Metal-covered hands

SPIDER-MAN

Friendly neighborhood wall-crawler

When Tony Stark is ordered to apprehend Captain America, Bucky Barnes, and the fugitive Avengers during the Avengers' Civil War, he needs a secret weapon. Stark recruits Midtown High School student Peter Parker. Parker was bitten by a radioactive spider that gave him arachnid abilities. He takes the name Spider-Man and pledges to help the weak.

It's a rare person that can steal Captain America's shield. Spider-Man manages this feat, proving himself to everyone.

WEB-SLINGER

Spider-Man's acrobatics make him a formidable opponent. He hitches a ride with War Machine, using his webs to fly into battle.

Detachable mask

Emotive eyes

Web line

Web-shooters

SPIDEY SUIT

Peter Parker creates a homemade Spider-Man suit and invents his own web fluid and web-shooters. Stark gives him an improved, high-tech version of the suit, equipped with an A.I. and more settings than Parker can remember.

Suit automatically adjusts for snug fit

Spider symbol and detachable drone

IRON SPIDER

Spider-Man in space

When Spider-Man tries to single-handedly rescue Doctor Strange, he gets caught on a ship headed into space. Thankfully Tony Stark always has a back-up plan and sends Spidey an upgrade: the Iron Spider suit. Parker then helps Strange, Stark, and the Guardians of the Galaxy face off against the warlord Thanos.

NEWEST AVENGER
Peter Parker is loyal to Tony Stark, although he doesn't always listen to him. As Iron Spider, he defies Stark's orders and rescues Doctor Strange—a daring act, after which he is welcomed into the Avengers.

Mechanical spider arms

Arms generated by nanotech

EIGHT LEGS
Iron Spider's legs are controlled by an A.I. They anticipate his needs by aiding climbs and softening impacts.

Precision claws can handle web lines

Iron Spider fights Thanos on Thanos's homeworld, Titan. Things don't go so well for Iron Spider.

Gauntlet protects web-spinners

Smart suit lets web lines out, but protects from incoming projectiles

DATA FILE
AFFILIATION: Avengers, Tony Stark
KEY STRENGTHS: Strength, speed, agility, durability, climbing, spider-sense, web-shooters. Iron Spider: four robotic legs, can survive in space
APPEARANCES: Captain America: Civil War, Avengers: Infinity War

EBONY MAW
Master manipulator

Ebony Maw is one of Thanos's adopted children. Gifted with the power of eloquent speech, he is also known as "The Maw." Maw speaks on Thanos's behalf when he destroys Gamora's homeworld. Maw is also tasked with recovering the Time Stone, but he gets sucked into space along the way.

Sparse white hair

MIND OVER MATTER

Maw is neither physically imposing nor in possession of a weapon. He doesn't need any because his powerful mind is capable of controlling the environment around him through telekinesis.

Armored tunic

TIME STONE QUEST

Ebony Maw restrains Doctor Strange aboard his ship. He hopes to force Strange to hand over the Time Stone before they reach Thanos on his homeworld, Titan.

Hands direct telekinetic powers

DATA FILE

AFFILIATION: Thanos
KEY STRENGTHS: Telekinesis, levitation, skilled manipulator
APPEARANCES: Avengers: Infinity War

CORVUS GLAIVE

Deadly tactician

Corvus Glaive is one of Thanos's adopted children. Glaive helps Thanos conquer worlds and acquire the powerful Infinity Stones. His mission on Earth is to recover the Mind Stone from the Avenger Vision, but Glaive is injured in Scotland and later perishes in Wakanda.

Hood shields skin from light

Elf-like earpiece

Glaive's weapon is so resilient it can deflect energy beams fired by the Mind Stone without taking damage.

CROW-BLADE

Glaive gets his name from his stealthy birdlike movements (the corvus species of birds includes crows) and his weapon. His powerful sword, known as a glaive, can pierce Vision's body and prevent him from phase-shifting.

FIERCE FOE

Corvus Glaive is a powerful fighter. On his quest to obtain the Space Stone for Thanos, Glaive boarded an Asgardian ship and took down most of the crew himself.

Cowl with gold detailing

Flexible body armor

DATA FILE

AFFILIATION: Thanos
KEY STRENGTHS: Strength, speed, durability, extraordinary weapon
APPEARANCES: Avengers: Infinity War

PROXIMA MIDNIGHT

The Spear of Thanos

Proxima Midnight is sent by her "father," Thanos, to recover the powerful Mind Stone from Vision. She and her mate, Corvus Glaive, stalk Vision and Wanda Maximoff from Europe to Africa. Proxima leads Thanos's Outrider army against Wakanda, but meets her end on the battlefield.

Horns grow from temples

WEAPONS MASTER

Proxima Midnight is skilled in hand-to-hand combat. Her preferred weapon is a three-pronged spear that fires bolts of energy. She also wields a sword and blades in her wrist gauntlets.

Reinforced torso armor is light for flexibility

Heavy armor on arms for close combat

OUTNUMBERED

Proxima and Corvus Glaive corner Vision and Wanda Maximoff at a train station in Edinburgh, Scotland, but Steve Rogers intervenes, forcing the villains to flee.

In Wakanda, Proxima attacks Wanda Maximoff, but Okoye and Black Widow come to Wanda's aid.

Stretch armor glove

Double-edged sword

DATA FILE

AFFILIATION: Thanos
KEY STRENGTHS: Strength, agility, speed, hand-to-hand combat
APPEARANCES: Avengers: Infinity War

CULL OBSIDIAN

Brute of Thanos

One of the children of Thanos, Cull Obsidian is large and terrifying. The beast gets his name from how effective he is at brutally reducing populations who have been conquered by Thanos. Cull joins the hunt for Earth's two Infinity Stones, but he is beaten by Bruce Banner in the Battle of Wakanda.

PULLED AWAY

Cull Obsidian battles Tony Stark in New York City, allowing Ebony Maw to retrieve the Time Stone from Doctor Strange.

Skull protected by natural armor

UNUSUAL WEAPON

Cull Obsidian's unique weapon has many functions. It can fire a projectile on a chain and transform into a shield.

Bandolier holds spare hammer blades

DATA FILE

AFFILIATION: Thanos

KEY STRENGTHS: Strength, durability, cybernetic arm, unusual weaponry

APPEARANCES: Avengers: Infinity War

Shapeshifting weapon

Hand later replaced with prosthetic

Powerful legs

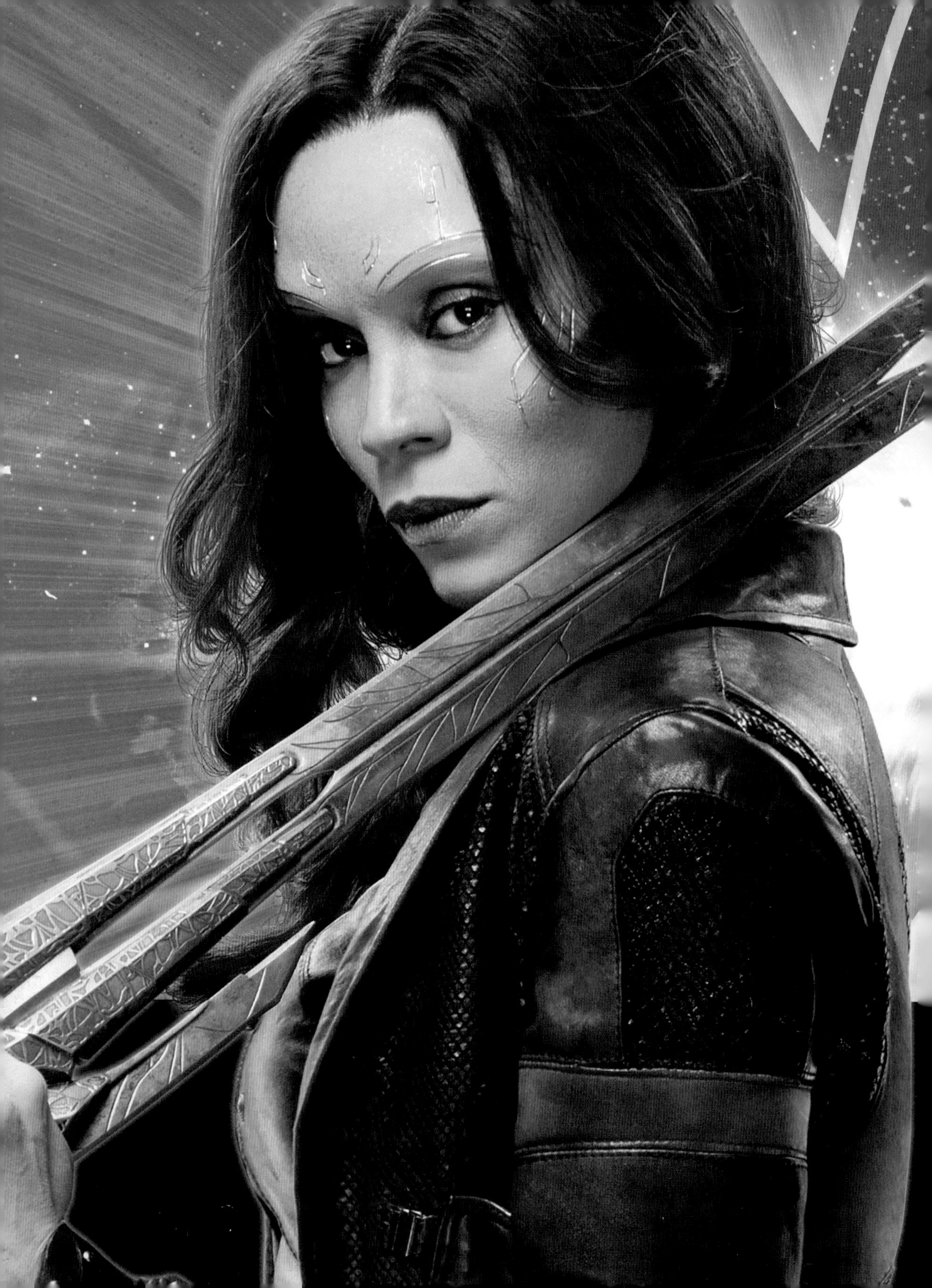

GUARDIANS OF THE GALAXY

Unlikely heroes with nothing in common—except that they have nothing to lose—band together to save the galaxy. The Guardians begin by taking on a small mission, but this leads to a confrontation with Thanos, a mad warlord, intent on destroying half the universe.

STAR-LORD

Legendary outlaw

Peter Quill is the son of Meredith Quill, a human, and the Celestial being known as Ego. Ego hires pirate Yondu Udonta to capture young Quill, but Yondu raises Quill as a Ravager pirate instead. Known also as the outlaw Star-Lord, Quill recovers a mysterious Orb. This sets him on a collision course with his future team, the Guardians of the Galaxy.

TEAM LEADER

Quill is a survivor. He navigates the galaxy by keeping an open mind and constantly adapting. His determination and easy acceptance of others make him a great leader of the Guardians. Also, he owns their ship, *The Milano*.

DATA FILE

AFFILIATION: Guardians of the Galaxy
KEY STRENGTHS: Unconventional thinking, pilot, unique space helmet
APPEARANCES: Guardians of the Galaxy, Guardians of the Galaxy Vol. 2, Avengers: Infinity War

Leather Ravager jacket

Quadblaster holster

Dual-trigger Quadblaster

Quill and Rocket fight for control of the ship. Rocket is actually the superior pilot.

UNLIKELY TEAM

Star-Lord's misfit team is formed in prison. They join forces to escape and deliver the Orb to The Collector, but end up fighting Ronan the Accuser.

Jet boots work for short distances

Jet boot controls are easy to access

GAMORA

Daughter of Thanos

Gamora is the adopted daughter of the tyrant Thanos. Thanos wiped out half her planet's population, but took pity on her. Gamora and her adopted sister, Nebula, trained together to become assassins. However, Gamora rebelled against Thanos and joined the Guardians of the Galaxy instead.

Sword splits into two long blades and a knife

Thanos does love his daughter Gamora, in his own twisted way. Gamora's feelings are complicated.

Cybernetic skeleton built on a metal spine

DATA FILE

AFFILIATION: Thanos, Guardians of the Galaxy

KEY STRENGTHS: Master assassin, martial arts, speed, agility

APPEARANCES: Guardians of the Galaxy, Guardians of the Galaxy Vol. 2, Avengers: Infinity War

NO FEAR

Gamora rushes to face her foes without fearing for her own safety. Her only concern is for others—and that Thanos will use her knowledge to eliminate half the universe.

BUILT TO RUN

Thanos fitted Gamora's body with cybernetic upgrades, which grant her unnatural athletic abilities. Nanomachines in her blood increase reaction time and healing.

Peter Quill is jealous when Gamora admires Thor. He shows off, hoping to regain her attention.

Springy heel aids jumping

ROCKET

Scavenger specialist

Once a creature known as 8P913, Rocket was genetically enhanced to possess extreme intelligence and the ability to speak. His bitter personality led to a life of crime. When Rocket and his best friend, Groot, are incarcerated at the Kyln prison, they team up with a group of fellow inmates to escape, and later become the Guardians of the Galaxy.

Hates having ears touched

"Vicki" BA-17 ion pistol

RACCOON LIFE
Rocket makes a lot of jokes and sometimes has fun at the expense of others. But deep down, he is afraid that people will think he is a monster. He admits that he never asked to be turned into a talking raccoon—it was done to him years ago.

DATA FILE

AFFILIATION: Groot, Guardians of the Galaxy, Thor
KEY STRENGTHS: Weapons expert, piloting, highly aggressive, strong survival instinct
APPEARANCES: Guardians of the Galaxy, Guardians of the Galaxy Vol. 2, Avengers: Infinity War

Clothing stolen from a space mall

Anti-chafing pad

Harness strap

Pockets full of ammo

"Katie" BN1 blaster

BROTHERS IN ARMS
Rocket and Yondu bond during their brief time together. Yondu sees a lot of himself in Rocket. Both push people away to hide their own shortcomings and regrets.

Rocket loves big, dangerous weapons. It's partly why he accompanies Thor to get a new hammer; so he can see the arsenals on Nidavellir.

GROOT

I am Groot!

Groot is kind-hearted, so it's surprising that he and Rocket are best friends, working as mercenaries. They accept a job hunting Peter Quill, but end up in prison instead. There they team up with Quill, Gamora, and Drax to form the Guardians of the Galaxy and stop Ronan the Accuser from obtaining a precious Infinity Stone.

Moss grows on upper body

CRIMINAL RECORD

When Groot is scanned at the Kyln prison, his rap sheet reveals he is a sentient plant (*Flora colossus*) from Taluhnia with three counts of grievous bodily harm on his record.

A NEW GROOT

Groot can regenerate from dramatic injuries, but some are so severe that he must start over. Groot is destroyed when he grows into a protective barrier around his friends, but Rocket finds a surviving cutting and regrows him.

Limbs regrow quickly when detached

Hands can release bioluminescent spores

Hand grows rapidly to skewer enemies

Legs can grow longer at will

DATA FILE

AFFILIATION: Rocket, Guardians of the Galaxy
KEY STRENGTHS: Rapid growth (healing and regeneration), physical strength, durability
APPEARANCES: Guardians of the Galaxy

Rocket and Groot work well together. They know each other's moves as they escape from prison.

BABY GROOT

I am Groot!

After Groot sacrifices himself to save his friends, Rocket salvages a Groot twig and plants the cutting. The potted plant grows into a cute new baby Groot who soon uproots himself and becomes a lovable but pesky member of the crew. Baby Groot loves music and dancing, but hates hats and Orloni space rats.

Moss grows atop head

Even dangerous situations are playtime for Groot. He dances while the Guardians fight the Abilisk monster.

Groot likes to eat his own leaves

RAVAGER ESCAPE

The Ravagers dress Groot in a tiny Ravager uniform. After their escape from Yondu's furious crew, Groot watches Rocket as he plans their flight course to Ego.

PINT-SIZED PLANT

Groot's feisty attitude and poor English comprehension skills make him hard to manage at times, but his small size comes in handy when the Guardians need to fit in tight places.

The Guardians depend on Groot to deliver a bomb to Ego's core, but he has trouble remembering instructions.

ADOLESCENT GROOT

I am Groot!

Baby Groot grows quickly into a moody adolescent. Groot's focus now is his game pad, purchased for him at a spaceport—and something Rocket soon regrets. He barely gives the other Guardians a glance, except to offer sarcastic comments and foul language. Still, deep down he is the same lovable "Twig."

Head rarely looks up from games

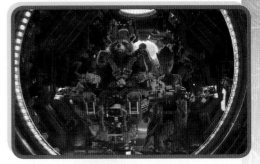

Groot splits from the Guardians to go with Thor and Rocket to Nidavellir. They hope to get a new weapon for Thor.

Long, spindly limbs

Torso composed of bark plates

DATA FILE

AFFILIATION: Rocket, Guardians of the Galaxy, Thor

KEY STRENGTHS: Rapid growth (healing and regeneration), physical strength, durability, extendable arms

APPEARANCES: Guardians of the Galaxy, Guardians of the Galaxy Vol. 2, Avengers: Infinity War

Bark smells like cedar and nutmeg

FORGING STORMBREAKER

Groot spends the entire adventure with Thor playing video games ... until he is needed most. He extends his own arm to grab the hot Uru metal and form the handle of Thor's Stormbreaker hammer—at great pain to himself.

BUDDING HERO

In his heartwood, Groot is grown from the same hero who once saved the Guardians. Though he is distracted most of the time, Groot fights alongside Thor and Rocket when he is truly needed.

DRAX

The Destroyer

Drax the Destroyer carries a deep sadness inside him. After his family was wiped out by Thanos, Drax has been driven by the need for vengeance. This gets him sent to the Kyln Prison, where he teams up with other inmates to escape. Drax and the escaped inmates become the Guardians of the Galaxy to stop Thanos's lieutenant, Ronan.

Tribal scar tattoos

Thick skin is difficult to pierce

Drax meets Mantis on Ego's planet. The two hit it off, though he finds her physically unattractive.

Skin has high healing factor to counter injuries

DIRECT SPEECH
Drax's people speak in a literal way and don't understand sarcasm, figures of speech, puns, or jokes. They tend to keep their emotions in check—except for rage. This can lead to some unfortunate misunderstandings.

Tribal dagger inside scabbard

NO SURRENDER
Drax has tremendous courage, self-confidence, and determination. He fearlessly runs at his enemies with blades ready, and is undaunted when Ronan or Thanos simply cast him aside.

DATA FILE
AFFILIATION: Guardians of the Galaxy
KEY STRENGTHS: Physical strength, agility, rapid healing
APPEARANCES: Guardians of the Galaxy, Guardians of the Galaxy Vol. 2, Avengers: Infinity War

Padded gladiator-style boots

YONDU UDONTA

Ravager pirate

Yaka energy streak

Prototype controller fin for Yaka arrow

Armor-piercing Yaka arrow

Yondu is a pirate-smuggler-criminal who is hired to kidnap young Peter Quill by a mysterious being named Ego. Instead of delivering him to Ego, however, Yondu raises Quill as part of his Ravager pirate crew. When Quill double-crosses Yondu, Yondu places a bounty on his head, but the pair's close bond means they eventually make up and join forces.

RISE OF THE RAVAGER

Yondu spent 20 years as a Kree battle slave. After gaining freedom, he joined a crew of Ravager pirates, led by Stakar Ogord. When shunned by Stakar for kidnapping young Peter Quill, Yondu forms his own crew of Ravagers aboard the *Eclector*.

WHISTLING WARRIOR

Yondu's whistles are converted into directional commands by his cranial controller fin. These are then transmitted to his Yaka arrow, which flies across the battlefield as required.

Blue Centaurian skin

DATA FILE

AFFILIATION: Ravagers, Peter Quill, Guardians of the Galaxy
KEY STRENGTHS: Owns a ship, commands a Ravager crew, deadly Yaka arrow
APPEARANCES: Guardians of the Galaxy, Guardians of the Galaxy Vol. 2

Ravager boot polished in Hoojib oil

Yondu sees Peter Quill as his own son, so he chooses to sacrifice himself to save Quill's life.

RONAN THE ACCUSER

Rogue warlord

On a mission of revenge against his ancient enemies on the world of Xandar, Kree warlord Ronan the Accuser makes a deal with the dangerous tyrant, Thanos. If Ronan can deliver a mysterious Orb to Thanos, Thanos promises to help him destroy Xandar. However, when Ronan realizes the Orb contains a mystical Infinity Stone, he decides to keep it for himself.

Accuser cowl covers bald head

WILLFUL WARMAKER

The Kree are superhumanly strong and their bodies can heal from even the most severe injuries. Ronan has lived for centuries and seen his family destroyed by the Xandarians.

DATA FILE

AFFILIATION: Thanos, Kree Empire, Korath, Nebula
KEY STRENGTHS: Strength, durability, war hammer wielding Infinity Stone, Sakaaran forces
APPEARANCES: Guardians of the Galaxy, Captain Marvel

Adapter able to contain Infinity Stone

Cosmi-Rod

Traditional Kree battle armor

With the Infinity Stone mounted on his Cosmi-Rod, Ronan has the ability to destroy planets like Xandar.

MISPLACED FAITH

On board his ship, *Dark Aster*, Ronan is informed by his ally Korath that an outlaw known as Star-Lord is in possession of the Orb. Ronan sends Gamora, one of Thanos's adopted daughters, after him.

Kree "skull-crusher" battle boots

Krehalium-plated war apron

NEBULA

Conflicted cyborg

Nebula is one of several adopted daughters of Thanos. She hates him for forcing painful cyborg upgrades on her body. She sides with Ronan against Thanos, but when he is defeated she goes on the run. Nebula is captured by the Sovereign people and delivered to the Guardians, leading to a reconciliation with her sister, Gamora.

Natural blue Luphomoid skin

Head plate protects brain

Ravager crew uniform

Arm houses whiplash and blaster

Fiber-reinforced hydrogel fabric

Shock-absorbing boots

DATA FILE

AFFILIATION: Thanos, Ronan, Ravagers, Guardians of the Galaxy, Gamora

KEY STRENGTHS: Strength, speed, endurance, agility, rapid self-repair

APPEARANCES: Guardians of the Galaxy, Guardians of the Galaxy Vol. 2, Avengers: Infinity War

Nebula undergoes relentless training and is a fierce hand-to-hand combatant. She prefers fighting with twin electroshock staffs.

SIBLING RIVALRY

Gamora and Nebula trained together as children. Thanos made them fight, punishing Nebula whenever she lost by slowly replacing her body with cyborg parts. He hoped it would improve her, but it only made her bitter.

SISTER'S SYMPATHY

Thanos captures Nebula and uses her pain to pressure Gamora into revealing the Soul Stone's location. Although Gamora denies knowing where it is, Thanos replays Gamora's own confession from Nebula's memory banks.

KORATH

Ronan's lieutenant

Korath the Pursuer is a Kree agent who volunteered for an experimental weapons program. He trains with Nebula and Gamora, and like them he undergoes cybernetic enhancements, as well as genetic alterations. Korath serves Ronan during the Kree-Skrull War, and again in his pursuit of the Orb and subsequent attack on Xandar.

SERVANT AND ADVISOR

Korath serves Ronan, but he respects and fears Thanos. When Ronan turns against Thanos, Korath is shocked and warns his master of the severe consequences.

Artificial neural network

FALLEN SOLDIER

Korath commands a platoon of Sakaaran soldiers. He is a skilled combatant but he is no match for Drax, who bests him aboard the *Dark Aster* ship.

N20-75 Disruptor Rifle

DATA FILE

AFFILIATION: Ronan the Accuser, Nebula

KEY STRENGTHS: Weapons and combat training, cyborg implants, military command

APPEARANCES: Guardians of the Galaxy, Captain Marvel

Orb of Morag

Custom-designed Kree armor

KRAGLIN OBFONTERI

Pirate deputy

Yondu Udonta's first mate, Kraglin, is a lifelong Ravager pirate. His frustration at Yondu's constant excuses for Peter Quill's selfish behavior inadvertently inspire a mutiny led by fellow Ravager, Taserface. When all goes horribly wrong, Kraglin helps Yondu, Rocket, and Groot escape and travels with them to help Quill and the Guardians defeat Ego.

Cheap Contraxia haircut

PASSING THE ARROW

Kraglin is a mostly faithful member of Yondu's crew and even mentors Peter Quill at times. Kraglin inherits Yondu's Yaka arrow after his captain's courageous death.

Shabby Ravager uniform

Holster harness

TOUGH CHOICES

Kraglin pilots the *Eclector* to rescue the Guardians from Ego's planet. Drax and the crew get on board but Kraglin is forced to leave Quill and Yondu behind.

Disruptor pistols

Kraglin feels the effects of 700 quadrant jumps to reach Ego's planet.

DATA FILE

AFFILIATION: Ravagers, Yondu, Guardians of the Galaxy
KEY STRENGTHS: Loyalty, piloting
APPEARANCES: Guardians of the Galaxy, Guardians of the Galaxy Vol. 2

EGO

Living planet

Ego is a Celestial, one of the oldest beings in the universe. His origins are mysterious, beginning as a brain-like being floating in space. Over eons he formed a planet around himself and created bodies to visit other worlds and spread his essence throughout the galaxy. He has created many children, although his Earth son, Peter Quill, is unique.

DATA FILE

AFFILIATION: Mantis, Peter Quill
KEY STRENGTHS: Power to evolve, rebuild himself, and spread to other worlds
APPEARANCES: Guardians of the Galaxy Vol. 2

CONFIDENCE GAME
Ego pretends to be a loving father to gain Quill's confidence, but his intentions are wholly evil. He only needs his son to amplify his power, much like a spare battery.

Ornately-carved silver bracers

Noble-looking robe

Leather belt and holster

Knee-high boots

SPREADING SEEDS
Ego's human form can only sustain itself for a short time when it travels away from his planet. So he seeds pieces of himself on worlds across the galaxy to create permanent outposts to which he can further expand his mind.

Ego forms a planet around his core. It takes on his personality and face, which is visible from space.

MANTIS

Empathetic explorer

Mantis is a naïve and kindly insectoid woman who befriends the Guardians of the Galaxy when they visit Ego's world. Mantis was raised by Ego after he found her as a larva, orphaned on her homeworld. She is able to sense others' feelings. Mantis uses her powers to help Ego sleep, but later turns against his evil plans.

Empathetic powers make antennae glow

Green and black insect-like clothing

DATA FILE

AFFILIATION: Ego, Guardians of the Galaxy
KEY STRENGTHS: Empathic (ability to sense feelings), can induce deep sleep in others
APPEARANCES: Guardians of the Galaxy Vol. 2, Avengers: Infinity War

NEW GUARDIAN

Mantis becomes a valuable member of the Guardians crew, using her powers not only to subdue Ego, but also to briefly interrupt Thanos in his effort to seize the Time Stone from Doctor Strange.

Petal-like openings in sleeves

Empathetic powers activated through touch

Coat tails resemble wings

MAKING FRIENDS

Poor Drax doesn't rest well because of the terrible loss of his family. He is excited to learn about Mantis's ability to induce slumber—and instantly falls into a deep sleep.

Ego tricks Star-Lord into coming to his planet, but Mantis knows the god-like being's dark secret and warns Drax.

MARTINEX

Pirate first mate

Martinex is the first mate of a Ravager pirate clan run by the legendary pirate, Stakar Ogord. Martinex has been a member of the crew for a long time. The original crew also included Aleta Ogord, Charlie-27, Krugarr, Mainframe, and Yondu Udonta. After Yondu's banishment, the crew disbanded, but Martinex remained as Stakar's first mate.

Growing head crystals require occasional carving

Cold, hard stare matches steely resolve

JUST LIKE THE OLD DAYS

Martinex pays his respects at Yondu's funeral, along with the other Ravager clans. The unexpected reunion inspires Stakar and Martinex to reassemble their old pirate crew.

Insulated jacket maintains low body temperature

SOLID AS A ROCK

Martinex is a Pluvian. His species is composed of silicon-isotope crystals. This unique Pluvian physiology allows him to survive in extremely cold temperatures, and even in the vacuum of space. His body is more durable than a human's, but when damaged heals far more slowly.

Weapons satchel strap

DATA FILE

AFFILIATION: Ravagers, Stakar Ogord
KEY STRENGTHS: Long lifespan, expert thief, loyalty, resilience
APPEARANCES: Guardians of the Galaxy Vol. 2

TASERFACE

Ravager mutineer

Taserface is a member of Yondu's Ravager crew. His gnarled face appears terrifying, but Taserface tries hard—much too hard—to look cool. He thinks Yondu has grown soft so he revolts and imprisons his captain. Taserface shoves everyone who supports Yondu out the airlock, apart from Kraglin, Rocket, and Groot, which proves to be a fatal mistake.

Untidy mohawk

Bulging veins add to gruesome appearance

Hair braid runs along beard edge

DATA FILE

AFFILIATION: Ravagers
KEY STRENGTHS: Strong influencer among Ravager crew
APPEARANCES: Guardians of the Galaxy Vol. 2

Messy, stuck on bits of fur

Corroded harness buckle

Taserface's trusty blaster

SEEDS OF REBELLION

After seeing Yondu belittled at the Iron Lotus on Contraxia, Taserface grows unimpressed with his captain. He begins planning a mutiny with his fellow Ravagers.

The Ravagers hunt down Rocket for their Sovereign employers, but when Yondu refuses to hand him over, Taserface revolts.

RIDICULED

Taserface is not especially smart and nobody takes him seriously. Before his ship explodes, Taserface tries to exact revenge by relaying Yondu's coordinates to the Sovereign. But his contact there just laughs hysterically at his name!

AYESHA

High Priestess

The Sovereign people are renowned for their snobbish sense of superiority. Their High Priestess, Ayesha, represents them, but her interests are entirely selfish. She hires the Guardians of the Galaxy to stop the Abilisk monster, but when Rocket steals valuable Anulax batteries, Ayesha becomes obsessed with eliminating them for insulting her.

DATA FILE

AFFILIATION: : The Sovereign
KEY STRENGTHS: Sovereign military resources and funding, obsessive nature
APPEARANCES: Guardians of the Galaxy Vol. 2

The Sovereign have thousands of remote-controlled Omnicraft, and Ayesha loses them all chasing the Guardians.

Crown fused to Sovereign throne

Collar represents symbolic protection of the voice of her people

THE RISE OF ADAM
The Sovereign are genetically engineered in birthing pods. As her ultimate creation, Ayesha designs Adam with the sole purpose of destroying the Guardians of the Galaxy.

Naturally golden skin

FUTILE PURSUITS
Ayesha tries to destroy the Guardians using every means at her disposal, including a full fleet of Omnicraft and hiring Yondu's Ravagers to hunt them down. All her efforts fail, leaving Ayesha in trouble with the Sovereign Council.

Relaxed posture conveys supreme confidence

ABILISK

Battery-eating monster

The Guardians of the Galaxy are hired by the Sovereign people to exterminate the terrifying Abilisk. The tentacled inter-dimensional beast is a hungry hatchling who likes to feast on the Sovereign's Anulax batteries, which power their civilization. The Guardians are given custody of Gamora's sister, Nebula, as payment for completing the task.

DATA FILE

AFFILIATION: Sovereign
KEY STRENGTHS: Powerful tentacles, lots of teeth, thick skin, blasts from mouth
APPEARANCES: Guardians of the Galaxy Vol. 2

Eyes see radiation and spectral energy

New teeth grow continuously

ABILISK'S END

The Guardians look like they may lose this fight. Their weapons seem useless, until Gamora spots a wound and plunges her sword into the Abilisk's flesh.

Tentacle for feeding and propulsion

Hide grows thicker with age

WORLDS TRAVELER

The Abilisk possesses the unique ability to move between dimensions by tearing holes in space-time with focused blasts of quantum splatter-matter.

Having no success defeating the Abilisk, Drax leaps into its mouth, passing through rows of sharp teeth.

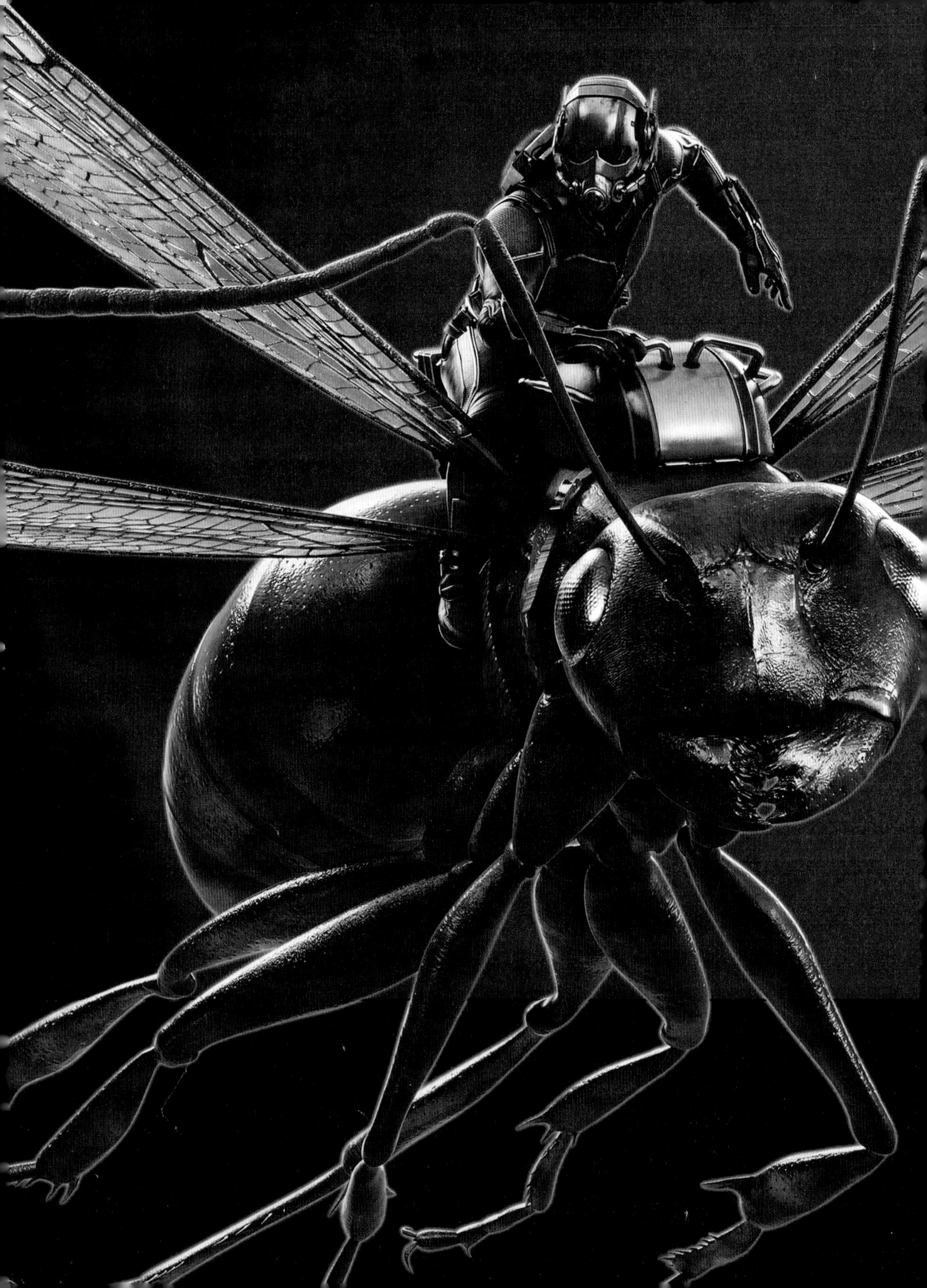

ANT-MAN

Thanks to the genius discoveries of scientist Hank Pym, Ant-Man and the Wasp can change size at will, slipping like insects into the lairs of corporate villains and high-tech criminals. However, when Ant-Man gets involved in the Avengers' squabbles, his problems get a lot bigger.

SCOTT LANG

Ex-con

Former criminal Scott Lang wants to get his life in order so he can spend time with his daughter, Cassie. But when his life falls apart, Lang teams up with scientist Hank Pym and his daughter, Hope van Dyne, to become a hero named Ant-Man. Together, they stop businessman Darren Cross from selling Pym's tech to terrorists.

Hank Pym tricks Lang into breaking into his house, where Lang steals the Ant-Man suit. Pym wants Lang to be the next Ant-Man.

HIGH-TECH THIEF

Scott Lang is a great burglar. He just isn't great at evading capture. Lang knows precisely what preparations are needed to blow even the most secure vaults.

Bath robe worn while under house arrest

HOUSE ARREST

Scott Lang is arrested after he violates the Sokovia Accords to help Captain America. He makes a deal to remain under house arrest for two years so he can be with his daughter, Cassie.

It takes creativity to keep from getting bored under house arrest. Lang plays the drums and learns to do magic tricks.

DATA FILE

AFFILIATION: Avengers, Hank Pym, Hope van Dyne, X-Con Security Consultants, Luis, Kurt, Dave, Captain America
KEY STRENGTHS: Determination, heart. Ant-Man: changing sizes, communication with ants
APPEARANCES: Ant-Man, Captain America: Civil War, Ant-Man and The Wasp

ANT-MAN
Insect-sized hero

Scott Lang is trained by Hank Pym and Hope van Dyne to use Ant-Man's varying size as an advantage. After defeating Darren Cross's Yellowjacket, Ant-Man joins some of the Avengers in resisting the Sokovia Accords. Later, he helps Hank and Hope find Janet van Dyne in the Quantum Realm ... before getting stuck there himself.

Anti-glare visor

Armor plated suit adapts to changing size

Ant-Man uses carpenter ants for fast transit, but seagulls keep eating his rides as he chases the gangster, Sonny Burch.

Regulator button

HATCHING ANT-MAN
When Scott Lang breaks into Hank Pym's vault, he expects to find a fortune. Instead he finds an Ant-Man suit, which he mistakes for a biker outfit.

Pouch contains vials of Pym Particles

UNDER CONTROL
Ant-Man changes size using Pym Particles, which are managed by buttons on his gloves and controls on his belt. His helmet prevents dangerous changes to his brain chemistry as he fluctuates in size.

Hope van Dyne isn't thrilled that Ant-Man got them all in trouble by fighting with the Avengers.

Ant-Man falls into the ocean while chasing Sonny Burch, before exploding in size to become the oversized Giant-Man.

DR. HENRY J. "HANK" PYM

The original Ant-Man

As a member of S.H.I.E.L.D., Hank Pym discovered Pym Particles, which can alter the size of any physical object. He also invented the Ant-Man suit. Hank and his wife Janet worked as a team to protect the world. When she was lost to the Quantum Realm, Pym founded his own company, Pym Tech, to find her, which he eventually does.

Superior and driven intellect

Professional attire reflects disciplined attitude

A NEW ANT-MAN

When rival genius Darren Cross takes control of Pym Tech and tries to replicate Hank Pym's technology, Pym convinces Scott Lang to wear the Ant-Man suit and help him stop Cross.

As the original Ant-Man and Wasp, Hank and Janet intercept a Soviet nuclear missile headed for the U.S.A. Janet halts it, but is unable to stop herself from shrinking.

FAMILY SECRETS

Pym devoted much of his life to finding his wife Janet. However, he keeps the nature of her disappearance a secret from his daughter, Hope, in a misguided effort to protect her.

DATA FILE

AFFILIATION: S.H.I.E.L.D., Janet van Dyne, Hope van Dyne, Scott Lang

KEY STRENGTHS: Scientific genius, Ant-Man technology

APPEARANCES: Ant-Man, Ant-Man and The Wasp

ANT-THONY

Small steed

Hank Pym keeps a lot of ants. Number 247 proves himself so loyal and friendly that Scott Lang gives him a name. "Ant-Thony" breaks Lang out of prison and transports him on several missions, including a break-in at the Avengers facility. He is tragically shot down while helping Lang escape Darren Cross.

ANT-TRANSPORT

Ant-Thony is a black carpenter ant. His species gets its name because they live in large colonies inside rotting wood. Ant-Man uses carpenter ants mostly for transport.

Saddle with handlebars

Four large wings for flight

Large mandibles for chewing wood

Six jointed legs

FLYING RESCUE

Ant-Thony flies Scott Lang from jail back to Pym's residence. Though Lang falls off along the way, Ant-Thony catches him and delivers him safely.

Scott Lang gives Ant-Thony a drink from a droplet of water. The two spend a lot of time training together.

DATA FILE

AFFILIATION: Ant-Man, Hank Pym
KEY STRENGTHS: Loyalty, bravery, flight, strength
APPEARANCES: Ant-Man

HOPE VAN DYNE

Pym Tech chairperson

The daughter of inventor Hank Pym, Hope's relationship with her father has always been strained by his refusal to tell the truth about her mother Janet's disappearance. Now chairperson of the Pym Tech board, Hope is manipulated into voting Pym out of his own company. They reconcile to stop the new CEO Darren Cross from selling Pym's technology to Hydra.

THE TRUTH

Hank doesn't want to place his daughter in danger, like he did her mother, so he pushes Hope away. When he finally tells her the truth (that her mother was lost during a mission as the Wasp) Hank gives Hope a suit of her own.

KEEPING ENEMIES CLOSE

Van Dyne keeps an eye on Darren Cross as he perfects size-changing Pym Particles. When he makes a breakthrough, Hope realizes that she must act now to stop him.

Tailored suit reflects high-powered board position

Van Dyne trains Scott Lang to be Ant-Man. Knowing that she is more qualified makes it frustrating for her at times.

DATA FILE

AFFILIATION: Pym Tech, Hank Pym, Scott Lang
KEY STRENGTHS: Business management. Wasp: fighting skills, communication with ants, size-changing ability, blasters, wings
APPEARANCES: Ant-Man, Ant-Man and The Wasp

Van Dyne helps her father search for her mother. She keeps everything running smoothly.

THE WASP

Tiny and mighty

Antenna boosts communication with insects

STING IN HER TAIL
Although Hank Pym could have equipped Scott Lang, he reserved a few exciting but dangerous features for his more capable daughter. In addition to her wings, Wasp's wrists can also fire powerful blasters.

Red tubing dispenses Pym Particles

Stinger blasters (also fires projectiles)

Pym Particle reservoir

Originally a title held by Janet Van Dyne, the Wasp is now Janet's daughter, Hope. The new Wasp partners with Ant-Man to recover Hank Pym's stolen lab and evade the FBI, gangster Sonny Burch, and the vengeful Ghost. The pair later build a quantum tunnel to rescue Hope's mother from the Quantum Realm.

Wasp uses her tiny size as an advantage when sneaking up on opponents.

TAKING FLIGHT
Wasp has wings of her own, so she has no need to ride carpenter ants like Ant-Man. Her four wings collapse into a compartment on her back when they aren't needed.

Lift-boosting boots

DARREN CROSS

Pym Tech CEO

A former protégé of Hank Pym, Darren Cross convinced Pym's daughter, Hope van Dyne, and the rest of the Pym Tech board of directors to vote Pym out of his own company. Cross is promoted as the new CEO and sets out to duplicate Pym's secret Ant-Man technology and sell it to terrorists.

Unbalanced, over-ambitious mind

Cross tests his experimental Pym Particles on lambs. It takes a while to perfect the technology.

OUTDOING PYM

Cross invites Hank Pym to the unveiling of his plans to develop Pym's Ant-Man technology. Pym is upset by the news, but Cross determines to outdo his mentor.

Expensive suit bought with CEO salary

PARANOIA

Cross is obsessed with Hank Pym's covert career as a S.H.I.E.L.D. agent and by his Ant-Man research. His fixation on Pym's secretive work isn't helped by the fact that Pym Particles have altered his brain chemistry.

DATA FILE

AFFILIATION: Pym Tech
KEY STRENGTHS: Ambition, determination. Yellowjacket: flight, lasers, strength, size-changing ability
APPEARANCES: Ant-Man

Hope van Dyne pretends to work with Cross in order to keep tabs on his scientific progress.

YELLOWJACKET

Ant-Man's enemy

Darren Cross succeeds at duplicating Hank Pym's Ant-Man research. He designs a weaponized suit for warfare called Yellowjacket, intending to sell it to the highest bidders (namely Ten Rings and Hydra). When Pym, his daughter Hope, and Scott Lang intervene, Darren Cross dons the Yellowjacket suit to fight Ant-Man.

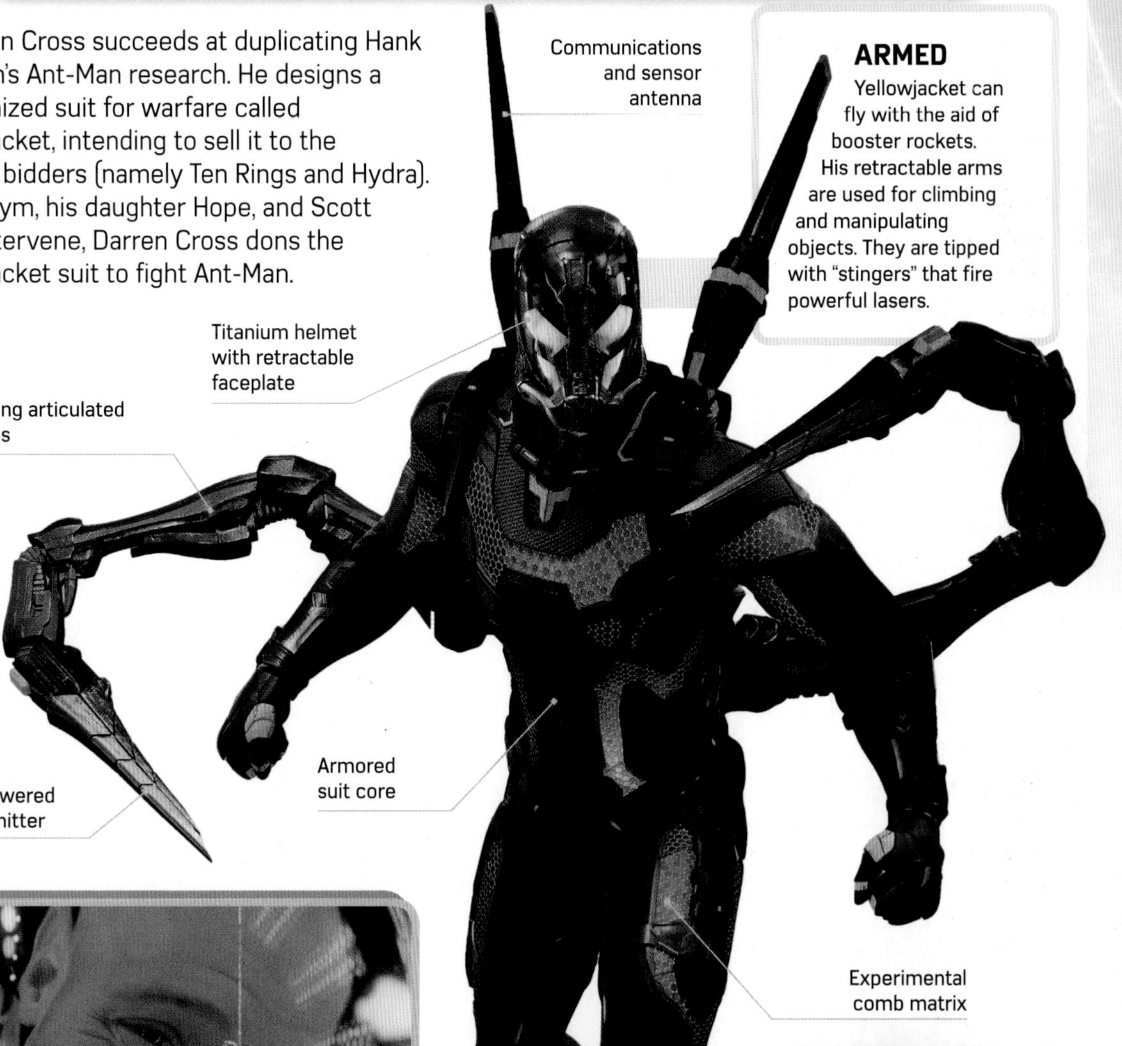
Communications and sensor antenna
Titanium helmet with retractable faceplate
Strong articulated limbs
High-powered laser emitter
Armored suit core
Experimental comb matrix

ARMED

Yellowjacket can fly with the aid of booster rockets. His retractable arms are used for climbing and manipulating objects. They are tipped with "stingers" that fire powerful lasers.

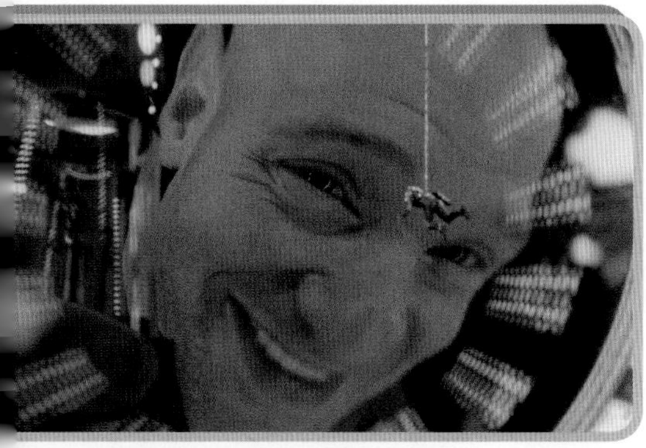

CAUGHT IN THE ACT

Darren Cross catches Ant-Man as he tries to steal the Yellowjacket suit. However, Cross's overconfidence gives Ant-Man an opportunity to escape and interfere with his deal with Hydra.

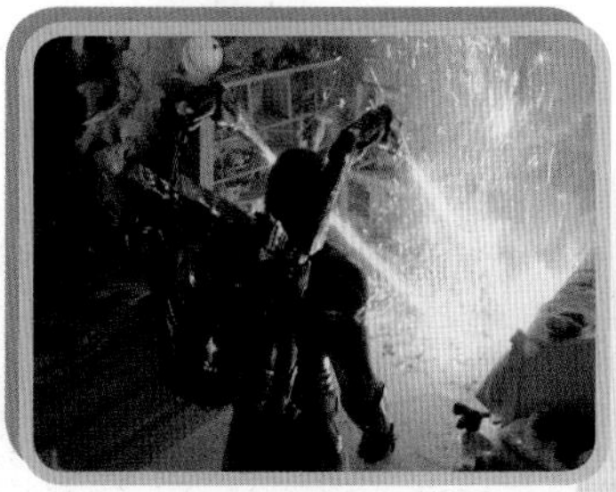

Yellowjacket blasts Ant-Man in his daughter, Cassie Lang's, bedroom. They shrink and grow as they battle.

CASSIE LANG

Devoted daughter

Cassie is the only child of Scott and Maggie Lang. Her parents are divorced so she mainly lives with her mom and Jim Paxton, Maggie's fiancé. This smart kid idolizes her father. She is his number one cheerleader, even when Scott disappoints her mom. Likewise, Cassie is Scott's motivation for reforming his own wayward life.

Keeps her hair long, just like her mom

Wears her dad's old shirt

WEEKENDS WITH DAD

After proving to Cassie's mom that he can be a good father, Scott gets to spend a lot of time with Cassie, even while he is under house arrest. She dreams about fighting alongside him as a hero.

Cassie would like to go on Ant-Man missions with her dad, but for now, they can only pretend.

DATA FILE

AFFILIATION: Maggie Lang, Scott Lang, Jim Paxton
KEY STRENGTHS: Smart, optimistic, capable
APPEARANCES: Ant-Man, Ant-Man and The Wasp

LIKE DAD, LIKE DAUGHTER

Sometimes Cassie faces Ant-Man's foes by herself. She is taken hostage by Yellowjacket and puts up a good fight until her dad arrives and defeats him.

JIM PAXTON

Strong stepfather

While Scott Lang is in prison, his ex-wife Maggie gets engaged to policeman Jim Paxton. Once Scott is released, Jim tries to keep him at a distance from Maggie and Scott's daughter Cassie. However, Scott convinces Jim that he's a good dad when he risks his life to save Cassie from Yellowjacket.

ANT-MAN FAN
Once he is won over, Jim has all criminal charges dropped against Scott. He is even supportive of Scott during his house arrest.

Always thinking of family first

COP AND CRIMINAL
Jim disapproves of Scott's criminal past and isn't impressed when Scott is arrested for robbing Hank Pym. He doesn't think Scott is a suitable influence on Cassie.

Cassie, Maggie, and Jim are surprised to see Scott as Giant-Man on TV, while watching as a family.

DATA FILE
AFFILIATION: Maggie Lang, Cassie Lang, San Francisco Police Department, Scott Lang
KEY STRENGTHS: Strong moral character, police training
APPEARANCES: Ant-Man, Ant-Man and The Wasp

LUIS

Business front man

Scott Lang's former cellmate from San Quentin State Prison is the jovial, optimistic Luis. After prison, the two live together and team up with fellow ex-criminals Kurt and Dave, using their skills to build a legitimate business. Friendly Luis loves telling rambling stories that often lead to trouble.

Favorite baseball cap

ASPIRING HERO

As a former criminal, Luis isn't used to being one of the good guys. He jumps at the opportunity to prove himself by helping his friend Scott foil corrupt businessman Darren Cross and then the super-powered Ghost.

X-Con onsite uniform

X-CON SECURITY CONSULTANTS

Luis, Kurt, Dave, and Scott use their expertise as former thieves to form a security agency. Luis is the face of the company while Scott is under house arrest.

Everyone is after Hank Pym's miniaturized lab. Luis tries to keep it from Ghost, Sonny Burch, and the authorities.

DATA FILE

AFFILIATION: X-Con Security Consultants, Dave, Kurt, Scott Lang, Hank Pym, Hope van Dyne
KEY STRENGTHS: Positive attitude, resourcefulness, loyalty
APPEARANCES: Ant-Man, Ant-Man and The Wasp

DAVE

Getaway driver

When Scott Lang gets out of prison, Luis introduces Scott to his friends, Kurt and Dave. An ex-con himself, Dave is the driver and car expert for the four during their heist at Hank Pym's house, and their break-in at Pym Tech. He continues to use these skills in their security company X-Con.

Company hat worn with attitude

CRIMINAL TO HERO
Dave dodges police as the team's getaway driver. When he and Kurt are seen on TV getting Burch to confess his crimes, it changes their image and boosts X-Con's business.

X-Con Security Consultants badge

LOOKOUT DUTY
Dave and Kurt keep watch while Luis, Scott, Hank, and Hope are inside Pym Tech, attempting to steal the Yellowjacket suit from Darren Cross.

Kurt and Dave help apprehend Sonny Burch and his thugs, who are trying to steal the Ant-Man tech.

DATA FILE

AFFILIATION: X-Con Security Consultants, Luis, Kurt, Scott Lang, Hank Pym

KEY STRENGTHS: Security expertise, expert driver

APPEARANCES: Ant-Man, Ant-Man and The Wasp

KURT

Tech expert

Kurt is a Russian hacker who ends up in Folsom State Prison for five years. Once released, he teams up with his friends Luis and Dave. They help Scott Lang, Hank Pym, and Hope van Dyne thwart criminals and gangsters, while also forming a security company of their own, called X-Con.

Kurt, Luis, and Dave speed around San Francisco trying to evade their enemies.

Contemporary Russian hairstyle

Anti-glare computer glasses

Laptop computer monitor

ASSEMBLING A TEAM

Kurt and Dave are introduced to Scott Lang while staying at Luis's apartment. The three convince a reluctant Scott to rob Hank Pym's house.

DATA FILE

AFFILIATION: X-Con Security Consultants, Luis, Dave, Scott Lang, Hank Pym

KEY STRENGTHS: Computer hacking skills, technology expert

APPEARANCES: Ant-Man, Ant-Man and The Wasp

TEAM HACKER

As the team's information technology specialist, Kurt is in charge of disabling security systems and supplying communications technology for their missions. He uses these same skills in their security company.

JANET VAN DYNE

The original Wasp

Janet is the wife of Hank Pym and the mother of Hope van Dyne. She used to work as the Wasp for S.H.I.E.L.D. alongside her husband, the original Ant-Man. Tragically, Janet was lost to the Quantum Realm when she shrank uncontrollably while deactivating a Soviet missile. Hank Pym has since devoted his life to rescuing her.

FAMILY FOUND

Janet contacted her family by planting information in Scott Lang's mind when he visited the Quantum Realm. Via a quantum entanglement, Janet was even able to speak through Scott.

Wasp suit

SURVIVING EXILE

Hank and his daughter, Hope, create a quantum tunnel to reach Janet. Hank finds her all alone. How Janet spent her 31 years in the Quantum Realm remains a mystery.

Mysterious, tattered cowl

Separated for decades, Janet is emotional at her reunion with her daughter, Hope.

DATA FILE

AFFILIATION: Hank Pym, Hope van Dyne, S.H.I.E.L.D.
KEY STRENGTHS: Compassion, resourcefulness, self-sacrifice, quantum particle manipulation
APPEARANCES: Ant-Man, Ant-Man and The Wasp

GHOST

Ava Starr

Ava Starr is the daughter of former S.H.I.E.L.D. agent Elias Starr. Her father steals quantum technology from Hank Pym and conducts tests that accidentally kill him and his wife in an explosion. Ava survives but her body is transformed, allowing her to shift between quantum dimensions and pass through objects.

Additional "eyes" assist vision during phase-shifting

TARGETS

Ghost acquires the location of Hank Pym, Scott Lang, and Hope van Dyne (along with Pym's lab) from Luis, who has been tied up and injected with truth serum by gangster Sonny Burch.

FAILING SUIT

S.H.I.E.L.D. trains Ava Starr as an assassin and Dr. Bill Foster creates a suit to help control her painful phase-shifting. However, it proves insufficient, so she plans to drain healing quantum energy from Janet van Dyne.

Vital organ stabilization chamber

Suit swipe controls

Phase-shifting buffer panels

Ghost uses her athletic skills to steal a motorcycle and chase the van carrying Hank Pym's miniaturized lab.

DATA FILE

AFFILIATION: Dr. Bill Foster, S.H.I.E.L.D.
KEY STRENGTHS: Quantum phase-shifting (invisibility and passing through objects)
APPEARANCES: Ant-Man and The Wasp

DR. BILL FOSTER

Rogue scientist

Dr. Bill Foster is a former S.H.I.E.L.D. agent. He worked with Hank Pym on Project G.O.L.I.A.T.H., where they experimented with Pym Particles to expand body mass. Foster achieved a height of 21 feet (6.4 meters), but left S.H.I.E.L.D after a falling out with Pym. The determined scientist secretly mentored a troubled young S.H.I.E.L.D. agent, Ava Starr (codename: Ghost), promising to cure her harmful quantum phase-shifting.

Retro academic glasses

QUANTUM SCIENTIST

Foster left S.H.I.E.L.D. before the rise of Hydra and became a professor at the University of California. There he teaches cutting-edge theoretical science.

Plain clothes deflect attention

DATA FILE

AFFILIATION: S.H.I.E.L.D., Hank Pym, Ghost
KEY STRENGTHS: Scientific expertise, compassion
APPEARANCES: Ant-Man and The Wasp

Foster works in a lab at Ava's hidden lair, trying to counteract the effects of her condition.

FOSTER'S GHOST

Foster and Ava have developed something of a father-daughter relationship over the years. Foster will do everything in his power to ease Ava's pain and save her life.

JIMMY WOO

FBI agent

Jimmy Woo is an accomplished FBI agent who serves as Scott Lang's law enforcement custodian after Lang violates the Sokovia Accords. Woo is also on the lookout for Hank Pym and Hope van Dyne, who violated the accords by originally providing Lang with the Ant-Man suit he wore while helping Captain America.

Perfectly groomed hair shows desire to be professional

SLEIGHT OF HAND
Though he is a dedicated FBI agent who relentlessly chases Lang, Pym, and van Dyne, Jimmy Woo is a good-natured guy. He is inspired by Lang's new hobby and tries to teach himself card tricks.

Freshly pressed regulation FBI suit

HOUSE SEARCHES
It is Jimmy Woo's job to make sure that ex-con Scott Lang stays at home and doesn't violate his house arrest. Lang does leave the house, but Jimmy is never able to catch him.

Polished FBI badge worn with pride

DATA FILE
AFFILIATION: FBI, Scott Lang
KEY STRENGTHS: FBI resources, dedication, integrity
APPEARANCES: Ant-Man and The Wasp

SONNY BURCH

High-tech smuggler

Shady gangster Sonny Burch has access to rare technology needed by Hope van Dyne to finish building the quantum tunnel. Hope tries to buy the component from Sonny, but he takes her money and refuses to hand it over. The stand-off leads to a fierce and ongoing struggle between Sonny and Wasp.

Slick manner masks a menacing streak

Garish, flashy tie

Cheap business suit

DESPERATE MEASURES

With the FBI after them, Hope van Dyne and her father must deal with smugglers like Sonny Burch to get the tech needed to build the quantum tunnel and find her mother.

Wanting to steal the quantum tunnel from Pym's lab, Sonny restrains Luis, Kurt, and Dave. He gives them truth serum to discover its whereabouts.

BAD BUSINESS

Sonny's untrustworthy practices make him an unreliable associate at best, and treacherous at worst. Most people only do business with him once.

DATA FILE

AFFILIATION: Criminal underworld
KEY STRENGTHS: Black market connections, gang resources, spies inside the FBI
APPEARANCES: Ant-Man and The Wasp

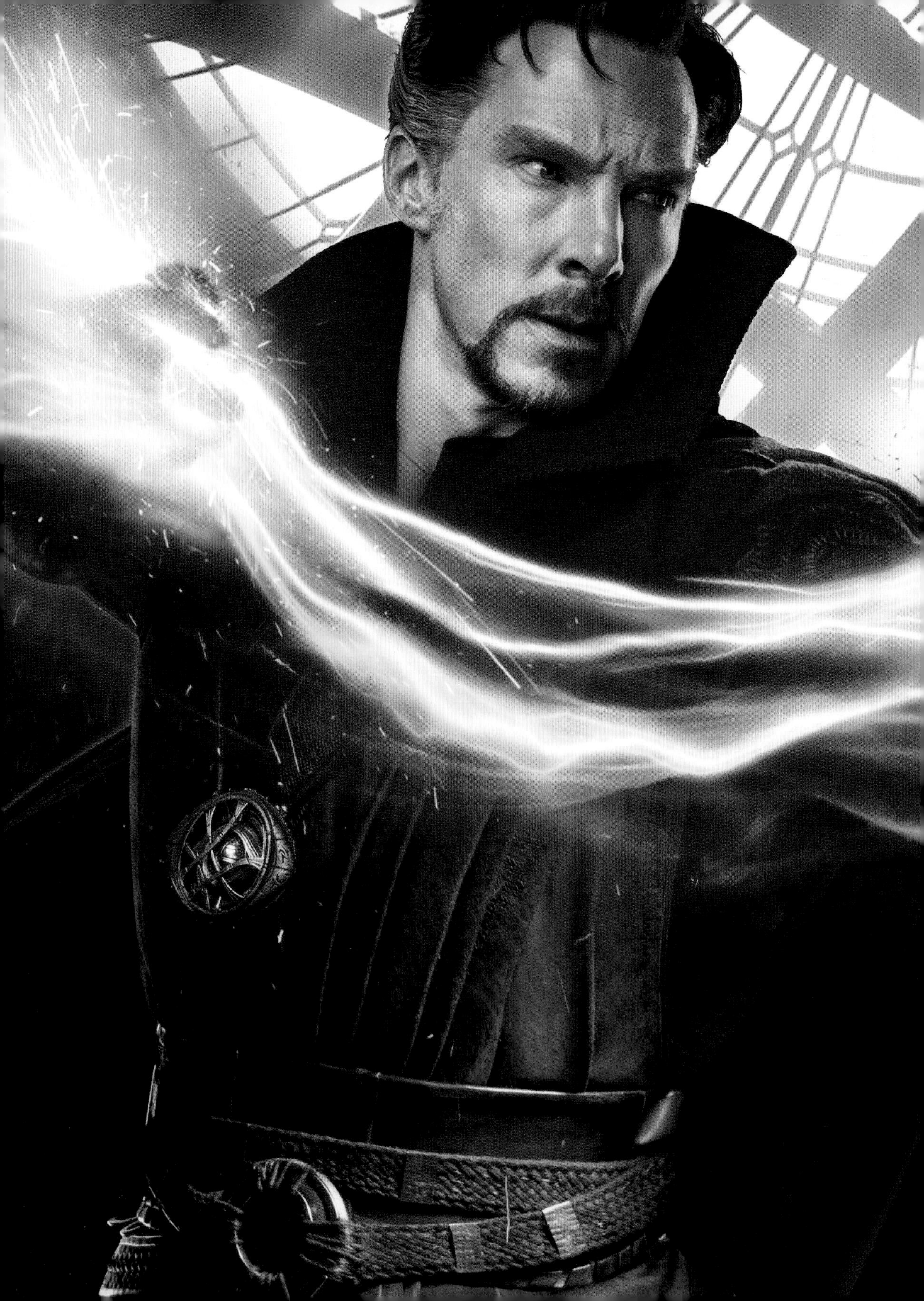

DOCTOR STRANGE

An arrogant doctor loses everything he cares about before finding new meaning as a Master of the Mystic Arts. As Doctor Strange, he battles evil sorcerers and extra-dimensional beings, while sworn to protect a mystical stone that controls time.

DR. STEPHEN STRANGE

Star surgeon

Stephen Strange is the best neurosurgeon in New York, until a terrible car accident leaves his hands damaged. He spends all his money trying to repair them and in desperation flies to Nepal, seeking a mysterious teacher known as "The Ancient One." There, he discovers a new direction for his life altogether.

Long, untrimmed hair

Scraggly beard

ARROGANCE
Strange entertains himself during surgery—and shows off—by playing games. As a surgeon he has a high success rate, though he declines cases he believes might fail.

SELF-DESTRUCTION
Strange is arrogant and proud. When he can't repair his hands, he lashes out in frustration and drives his love, Christine Palmer, away. He sacrifices everything in feeble hopes of regaining his old life.

Water-resistant jacket

Layered clothing for variable weather

The Ancient One shows Stephen Strange many strange dimensions in the Multiverse, including the Grass Jelly Dimension.

Travel guide and hand-drawn maps

Dirty, weathered pants

Strange practices trying to open a portal with a sling ring. He lags behind other students.

DOCTOR STRANGE

Master of the Mystic Arts

Stephen Strange studies at a place known as Kamar-Taj, becoming a Master of the Mystic Arts. When his teacher, The Ancient One, is killed by Kaecilius, Strange becomes the Sorcerer Supreme. From his base at the Sanctum Sanctorum in New York, Strange defends the Earth against supernatural threats, inter-dimensional beings, and alien forces.

Conjured shield

Eye of Agamotto

Strange tries to keep the Time Stone from Thanos by using strange spells, but ultimately he fails.

Cloak of Levitation

CHANGING TIME

Strange's early experiments with the mystical Eye of Agamotto scare his friends, Wong and Mordo. But the skills he gains controlling it allow him to defeat the terrifying Dormammu.

DATA FILE

AFFILIATION: Metro-General Hospital, Christine Palmer, Masters of the Mystic Arts, Wong, Avengers
KEY STRENGTHS: Intelligence, innovation, casting spells, Time Stone (Eye of Agamotto)
APPEARANCES: Doctor Strange, Avengers: Infinity War

STONEKEEPER

Doctor Strange is the keeper of the Eye of Agamotto. The magical relic is powered by an Infinity Stone known as the Time Stone, which allows the user to control all aspects of time.

DR. CHRISTINE PALMER

Fearless physician

New Yorker Dr. Christine Palmer is Stephen Strange's ex-girlfriend and colleague. She takes care of him after his accident, but in his self-centered frustration, Stephen pushes her away, resulting in a breakup. Thankfully Palmer has a forgiving nature and saves Strange's life when he is badly injured by Lucian, a follower of the villain Kaecilius.

Balancing their personal and professional relationships is challenging. Palmer knows firsthand how competitive and self-absorbed Strange is.

OUT OF BODY ADVICE

Doctor Strange advises Palmer from his ghostly astral body as she operates on his physical body. It's the first time she has seen him since he left for Kamar-Taj.

Hair pulled back in preparation for surgery

DATA FILE

AFFILIATION: Metro-General Hospital, Doctor Strange
KEY STRENGTHS: Medical training, compassion, loyalty
APPEARANCES: Doctor Strange

Regulation doctor's scrubs

Palmer attends to Strange's hands as he recuperates after his horrific car accident.

SMART CHOICES

Palmer is kind and compassionate, but she isn't a pushover. She walks away from Strange when he develops a poisonous attitude. It's a wise move because it gives him space to straighten out his life.

THE ANCIENT ONE
Sorcerer Supreme

The title of Sorcerer Supreme has been passed down for thousands of years, beginning with the Mighty Agamotto. "The Ancient One" has lived for centuries, teaching new Masters of the Mystic Arts from her home at Kamar-Taj. She is sworn to protect the Eye of Agamotto—and Earth—from supernatural threats.

Eyes bright with enlightenment

DATA FILE
AFFILIATION: Masters of the Mystic Arts, Doctor Strange
KEY STRENGTHS: Casting spells, wisdom, leadership, teaching, Dark Dimension powers
APPEARANCES: Doctor Strange

POWER OF DARKNESS
The Ancient One secretly draws her power from the Dark Dimension. She hates to rely on such a dangerous source, but must sustain her own life until she can train someone suitable to replace her.

Scarves can be weaponized with magic

Outstretched hands during levitation

Timeless, unusual clothing suggests she is from another time and place

Warm woolen underskirt

FINAL FIGHT
The Ancient One's weapons of choice are magical war fans. She conjures them to battle Kaecilius and his zealots in the Mirror Dimension, though he defeats her there.

The Ancient One teaches Doctor Strange the basics about casting spells in her Kamar-Taj classroom.

WONG

Librarian of Kamar-Taj

Master Wong is the strict librarian of Kamar-Taj. Wong is unsuccessful in his defense of the Hong Kong Sanctum against renegade mystic Kaecilius, but he stands with Doctor Strange against the evil Dormammu. Wong later serves Strange at the New York Sanctum, and guards it on his own when Strange is taken by one of Thanos's sons, Ebony Maw.

Intense focus before casting magic spell

WONG'S MAGIC WAND

Wong is a master of the Wand of Watoomb, an ancient relic with horned heads on each end. The baton allows the wielder to absorb, amplify, and redirect powerful magical energy.

Hands poised to conjure mystical shields

Doctor Strange and Wong look down upon Bruce Banner, who crashes through the ceiling, warning them of Thanos's arrival.

Well-used sling rings

Heavy garments protect against extreme cold

SACRED TEXTS

As librarian, Wong helps Strange select reading material. Wong remarks that no knowledge is off-limits ... just certain magical practices. Strange's studies progress quickly, however, as he borrows books without Wong's permission.

MORDO

Disenchanted sorcerer

Mordo came to Kamar-Taj seeking knowledge and power. Instead, the teachings of The Ancient One brought him balance and peace. When he learns that The Ancient One has been drawing her own power from the Dark Dimension, he becomes disheartened and leaves the order, resolving to rid the world of sorcerers.

Staff of the Living Tribunal

Hand always ready to fight or cast spells

HELPING HAND

Mordo observes Stephen Strange searching the streets of Kathmandu for the fabled Kamar-Taj. He intervenes when robbers trap Strange. After a scuffle, Mordo takes the desperate doctor to The Ancient One.

Elaborate handcrafted yak leather belt

DATA FILE

AFFILIATION: Masters of the Mystic Arts, Doctor Strange, The Ancient One
KEY STRENGTHS: Casting spells, martial arts skills
APPEARANCES: Doctor Strange

Layered wool cloak

Mordo tries unsuccessfully to teach Strange how to open a portal with a sling ring.

Vaulting Boots of Valtorr

A FITTING RELIC

According to legend, Mordo's magical staff once belonged to a powerful but aloof being who sat as a ruthless judge and sentenced guilty parties to horrific punishments. Mordo adopts that same uncompromising spirit in his own life.

KAECILIUS

Disciple of Dormammu

Mourning the loss of his family, Kaecilius comes to Kamar-Taj to find peace. He studies the Mystic Arts under The Ancient One, covertly looking for the power to bring his family back. When he learns his teacher is secretly drawing power from the forbidden Dark Dimension, he rebels and joins the destructive Dormammu.

Discolored skin from Dark Dimensional energy

BLIND AMBITION

Kaecilius and his followers perform a ritual to contact Dormammu and draw power from the Dark Dimension. He doesn't realize that the eternity promised by Dormammu is, in reality, endless torment.

Kaecilius battles Doctor Strange in the Mirror Dimension, where his own powers are greatly amplified.

Warm wool leggings

SORCERER'S FOLLY

Kaecilius steals forbidden knowledge from the Book of Cagliostro. He reads only the pages with spells, failing to heed the warnings. Though he does open a portal for Dormammu, Kaecilius is imprisoned in the Dark Dimension.

Concealed inner pockets to hide stolen relics

Boot covers protect from rain

DORMAMMU
Dreadful destroyer

The extra-dimensional being known as Dormammu is a destroyer of worlds. He is at home in the Dark Dimension and seeks to devour all other dimensions in the Multiverse. Dormammu's power is seemingly infinite. When he invades Earth, aided by his disciple, Kaecilius, Doctor Strange mounts a defense and eventually forces him to retreat.

Dormammu agrees to leave and never return—taking Kaecilius and his remaining followers with him to suffer eternal torment.

DORMAMMU'S DOOM

Dormammu uses Kaecilius to enable him to enter the world. He begins to swallow up the city and the very fabric of reality itself.

Consciousness rendered as green ectoplasm

Eyes emanate life force energy

TIME'S UP

Time does not exist in the Dark Dimension, which leaves Dormammu with no defense against Doctor Strange's clever strategy. Strange uses the mystical device known as the Eye of Agamotto to trap Dormammu in a time loop.

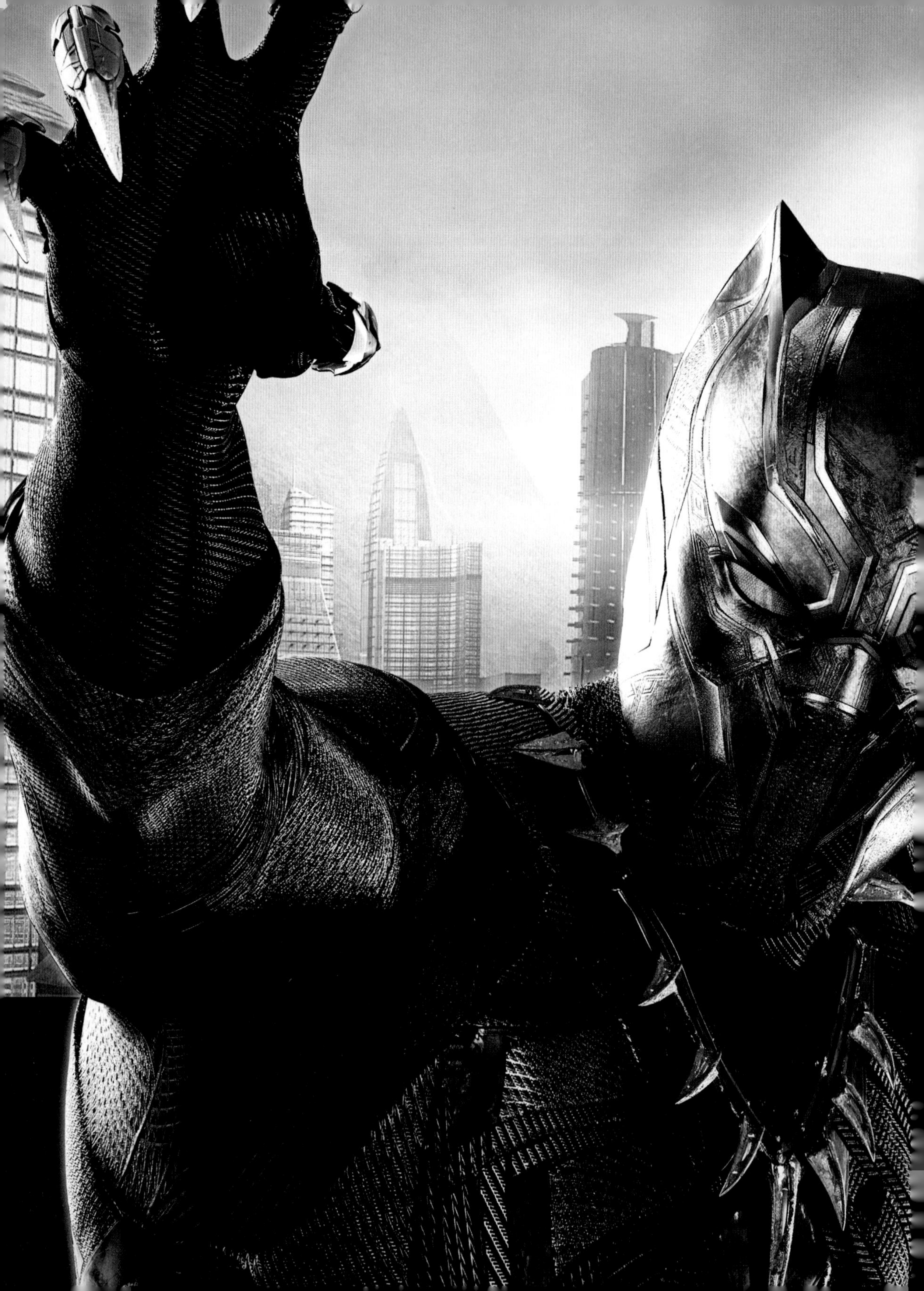

BLACK PANTHER

The African kingdom of Wakanda, hidden from the world, holds the secret to incredible wealth and conceals what might be Earth's greatest technological achievements. The Black Panther fights to protect Wakanda, but his greatest threat comes from within his own family.

T'CHALLA

King of Wakanda

T'Challa becomes the king of Wakanda after his father, T'Chaka, is killed by a terrorist bomb. The devoted son inherits the throne and vows to protect his kingdom. Together with his mother, Ramonda, and sister, Shuri, T'Challa faces challenges to his throne, his country, and his planet.

Erik Killmonger arrives in Wakanda to challenge T'Challa for the throne. T'Challa permits him entry, knowing that Killmonger is his cousin.

United Nations attire

SECRET KINGDOM

T'Challa hides his nation's technological prowess from the world by blanketing the capital city with a hologram. In this way, Wakanda masquerades as a developing country to protect itself from those that may wish to steal their powerful and advanced vibranium technology.

"From Wakanda, with Love" silk scarf

T'Challa rules Wakanda from a palace in the capital, where he is surrounded by a council of elders.

CHALLENGE CEREMONY

T'Challa accepts Killmonger's challenge and fights him without the benefit of his Black Panther powers. Killmonger has trained his entire life for this. He mercilessly throws T'Challa over the waterfall, ending his reign.

BLACK PANTHER

Proud protector

Generations of Wakandan kings have attained the legendary power of the Black Panther by drinking an elixir made from a secret heart-shaped herb. As the latest Black Panther, King T'Challa uses his super-human abilities to defend his people, with the aid of a remarkable black suit designed by his sister, Shuri.

Sensitive ear microphones

Solid vibranium accents

PANTHER SUIT
The Black Panther suit is woven with vibranium—Earth's rarest and strongest metal. The suit can store kinetic energy and redirect it for use in the next blow.

Flexible bulletproof material

PEOPLE'S PROTECTOR
The Black Panther must look after all Wakanda's subjects. He also wants to combat villainy around the world, which is why he decides to share advanced Wakandan technology with the United States.

Retractable vibranium claws

Fabric woven with vibranium

The Black Panther faces his nemesis Killmonger deep inside Wakanda's vibranium mine. They both wear a Black Panther suit, but T'Challa's victory is won using his own strength.

DATA FILE
AFFILIATION: Golden Tribe, Wakanda, Avengers, Tony Stark
KEY STRENGTHS: Physical strength, speed and agility, vibranium claws and shielding
APPEARANCES: Captain America: Civil War, Black Panther, Avengers: Infinity War

NAKIA

Conflicted hero

Wakanda's top spy, Nakia, is a member of the War Dogs, Wakanda's intelligence agency. She is also a princess of the River Tribe and the former girlfriend of Prince T'Challa. The brave and resourceful Nakia goes on dangerous undercover missions to Nigeria and across Africa, as well as overseas to countries like South Korea.

Ornate beaded necklace

Kimoyo bead acts as a medical device

KINDHEARTED

Nakia goes on missions far from Wakanda. She is frustrated by the way her country hides from the world rather than helping others in need. In doing so, she frequently puts herself in danger.

Vibranium chakram blade

Nakia and Okoye chase smuggler Ulysses Klaue through the busy streets of Busan, South Korea.

Green ceremonial dress celebrates traditional River Tribe color

FIERCE FIGHTER

Nakia is a skilled fighter, trained in martial arts. Always putting her country first, she wears the armor of the Dora Milaje, Wakanda's royal guard, when helping T'Challa fight Killmonger and the Border Tribe.

Knee length boots for formal attire

Nakia is thrilled when T'Challa agrees to open Wakanda to aid people from other countries.

DATA FILE

AFFILIATION: Wakanda, River Tribe, War Dogs, T'Challa
KEY STRENGTHS: War Dog training, espionage, fighting skills, intelligence
APPEARANCES: Black Panther

SHURI

Wakandan inventor

T'Challa's brilliant younger sister is a scientific genius who develops new vibranium technology, including remote controlled flying ships, advanced medical devices, and powerful weapons. Shuri helps T'Challa win back the throne of Wakanda from Erik Killmonger. She heals Bucky Barnes's troubled mind, and plays a crucial role in the battle against Thanos.

Blast fires from panther mouth

Vibranium armband

STAND STRONG

Shuri stands with her brother against the usurper Killmonger. Her vibranium gauntlets are strong, but their blasts are absorbed by Killmonger's suit.

Hand-carved belt buckle

Shuri, Ramonda, and the Dora Milaje await the arrival of T'Challa and Nakia in a Royal Talon Fighter.

HEAR MY ROAR

Shuri has an independent mind and a strong will. She often teases her older brother, the king, but she is his most trusted advisor. She also developed all of Black Panther's high-tech gear.

Lacquered vibranium finish

Gauntlets have single blast or continuous mode

DATA FILE

AFFILIATION: Wakanda, Golden Tribe, T'Challa
KEY STRENGTHS: Scientific genius, intelligence, creativity
APPEARANCES: Black Panther, Avengers: Infinity War

Shuri attempts to safely disconnect the Infinity Stone in Vision's forehead before Thanos finds him.

OKOYE

Wakandan warrior

Leadership
tattoo

Okoye is the personal bodyguard of King T'Challa and the fierce leader of the royal guard known as the Dora Milaje. She is also a personal friend and trusted advisor to the king. Okoye accompanies T'Challa on missions to other countries and defends Wakanda against the forces of Thanos.

LOYALTY

Okoye swore an oath to protect the king. When her husband W'Kabi betrays T'Challa she stands against him. Okoye's loyalty to Wakanda always comes first and she defends her beloved country with her life.

Gold-plated spear lock
connection point

When she learns T'Challa survived the Challenge Ceremony, Okoye turns against Killmonger to defend the true king.

DUTY FIRST

After Killmonger takes over, Nakia urges Okoye to flee with her, Ramonda, and Shuri. However, Okoye stays behind to defend the throne, no matter who sits on it.

Spear tip can control nearby electronic devices

DATA FILE

AFFILIATION: Wakanda, Dora Milaje, T'Challa
KEY STRENGTHS: Dora Milaje training, speed, agility, hand-to-hand combat with spear
APPEARANCES: Black Panther, Avengers: Infinity War

Electromagnetic soles

W'KABI

Border Tribe leader

DATA FILE

AFFILIATION: Border Tribe, Wakanda, T'Challa, Okoye, Killmonger
KEY STRENGTHS: Skilled fighter, controls Border Tribe army
APPEARANCES: Black Panther

W'Kabi's tribe lives in Wakanda's highlands where they raise livestock. W'Kabi is King T'Challa's best friend, but he loses faith in him when T'Challa fails to apprehend Ulysses Klaue, the man responsible for W'Kabi's father's death. When Killmonger gets the job done, W'Kabi sides with him against T'Challa.

RHINO RIDER

W'Kabi raises battle rhinos and summons them when T'Challa challenges Killmonger. The beasts charge through the Dora Milaje like battering rams, but unfortunately for W'Kabi, the rhinos love his wife, Okoye, who stops them in their tracks.

Border Tribe ritual markings on face

Border Tribe textiles contain shield projectors

W'KABI SHAMED

The Border Tribe is defeated by the Dora Milaje and W'Kabi surrenders when his wife Okoye confronts him. Though W'Kabi is a traitor, his tribe later helps the Black Panther fight Thanos's forces.

When W'Kabi allies himself with Killmonger against the true king T'Challa, it drives a wedge between him and his wife, Okoye.

Blanket incorporates Adinkra symbol of cooperation

ERIK KILLMONGER

Righteous rival

Erik Stevens, a.k.a. N'Jadaka, is the son of N'Jobu, the brother of Wakanda's former king, T'Chaka. When N'Jobu attacked Zuri, a friend of the royal family, T'Chaka killed him. Young Erik was abandoned in Oakland, California, where he devoted his life to taking revenge on the Wakandan royal family. He later takes the throne of Wakanda, declaring himself king.

Royal ring of grandfather King Azzuri

Killmonger uses a vibranium artifact at the Museum of Great Britain to gain Ulysses Klaue's confidence.

Fragmentation grenade

Daniel Defense DDM4 MK18 assault rifle

DATA FILE

AFFILIATION: Former member of Wakandan royal family
KEY STRENGTHS: Navy SEALs and Black Ops training, power of the Black Panther
APPEARANCES: Black Panther

Camouflage cargo pants

DEALER OF DEATH

Killmonger earns his menacing nickname because of his brutality. His body is covered in leopard-like scars that mark his victories. He deliberately seeks out the most dangerous missions to prepare himself for mortal combat against T'Challa.

KING NO MORE

Just when Killmonger thinks he is secure as Wakanda's new king, T'Challa returns. Killmonger dons an advanced Black Panther suit of his own and attacks.

ULYSSES KLAUE

Armed and ready

Klaue is a South African arms dealer and criminal. He worked with Prince N'Jobu to steal a fortune in vibranium from Wakanda. Klaue sold his share to Ultron, but lost his arm when Ultron lost his temper. He acquires a replacement prosthetic arm fitted with a vibranium sonic cannon. Klaue is betrayed by N'Jobu's son Killmonger when they team up to steal more vibranium.

Claw necklace over tattoo

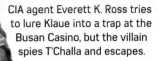

CIA agent Everett K. Ross tries to lure Klaue into a trap at the Busan Casino, but the villain spies T'Challa and escapes.

CRIMINAL RECORD

Klaue is a wanted man for crimes against Wakanda. He has already been caught stealing vibranium once, for which he was branded on his neck. Klaue is also responsible for the death of W'Kabi's parents in an explosion he caused at the Wakandan border.

Chamber conceals vibranium cannon

Cybernetic hand

Mix tape in pocket

ARMED AND DANGEROUS

The Black Panther, Okoye, and Nakia track down Klaue in Busan, South Korea, hoping to bring him to justice. Klaue uses the deadly sonic cannon concealed inside his synthetic arm to attack his pursuers.

DATA FILE

AFFILIATION: Killmonger, Ultron
KEY STRENGTHS: Cybernetic arm, underworld contacts
APPEARANCES: Avengers: Age of Ultron, Black Panther

M'BAKU

Jabari Tribe leader

The Jabari Tribe live in the highland peaks, far from the rest of Wakanda's people. M'Baku is the leader. His people shun the use of vibranium technology. M'Baku resents Wakanda's ruling family, but makes peace and comes to T'Challa's aid when Erik Killmonger threatens their nation's future, and again when Thanos invades.

Knobkerrie (club-staff weapon)

TRIBAL CONFLICT

M'Baku challenges T'Challa for the throne. Wearing a wooden mask to represent the White Ape, M'Baku fights fiercely at the Challenge Ceremony. He fails however, and leaves in peace.

Studded wood panels over fur gauntlets

DATA FILE

AFFILIATION: Jabari Tribe, Wakanda
KEY STRENGTHS: Hand-to-hand combat, physical strength, Jabari army
APPEARANCES: : Black Panther, Avengers: Infinity War

Natural grass skirt for warmth

Knee-cap protector

M'Baku's wooden palace is located high in the snowy mountains of Wakanda, isolated from other tribes.

THE GREAT GORILLA

The Jabari are vegetarians who wear rustic clothing made of natural materials. Their proud symbol is a primate—a striking contrast to the Black Panther. M'Baku is known throughout Wakanda as the "Great Gorilla."

AYO

Head of security

Ayo is the right hand of General Okoye and serves as the Dora Milaje Security Chief for King T'Challa of Wakanda. She stays close to the king on his travels around Wakanda and on overseas trips to Berlin and the United Nations. Ayo also bravely defends Wakanda in the battle against Thanos's forces.

Traditional Wakandan necklace

Vibranium spear can be electrified

HEROIC HEIRLOOM

The traditional costumes of the Dora Milaje are passed from mother to daughter. They feature leather harnesses with hand-stitching and detailed beadwork. Protective talismans hang from their intricate tabards.

Royal red tabard

Hand-tooled vibranium bracers

KING AND COUNTRY

As a member of the Dora Milaje, Ayo must watch T'Challa's Challenge Ceremony without interfering. When Killmonger is victorious, Wakandan law says she must protect him as king.

Ayo accompanies T'Challa, Nakia, and Okoye to the U.N., where the king opens Wakanda to the world.

RAMONDA

Queen Mother of Wakanda

Ramonda is the mother of King T'Challa and widow of King T'Chaka. She sits on the council of elders where she helps govern Wakanda. When T'Challa is thought to have died after his battle with Killmonger, she offers the mantle of Black Panther to M'Baku, but is overjoyed to learn from the Jabari Tribe leader that her son still lives.

Natural Wakandan sapphire pendant

ON THE RUN
When Killmonger seizes power after defeating T'Challa in ritual combat, Ramonda and Shuri flee for their lives. They meet Nakia and Everett Ross before looking to the loyal Jabari Tribe for help.

Kimoyo music beads

FASHION FUSION
Ramonda's striking fashion style, like her culture, is a careful blend of traditional Wakandan art and hyper-modern technology. Her distinctive and intricately designed hats are made with the aid of a 3-D printer.

Ramonda stands with her daughter Shuri for T'Challa's Challenge Ceremony. Pride is mixed with concern when M'Baku arrives.

Regal silk gown with dirt-repellent fibers

DATA FILE

AFFILIATION: Wakanda, T'Chaka, T'Challa, Shuri
KEY STRENGTHS: Complete dedication to family, duty to country, emotional strength
APPEARANCES: Black Panther

ZURI

Spiritual leader

Zuri is the high priest of Wakanda and a close friend to both T'Chaka and his son T'Challa. In his youth, Zuri was sent on an undercover mission for King T'Chaka to spy on his brother, Prince N'Jobu. During a confrontation, T'Chaka killed N'Jobu to save Zuri. Years later, Zuri is murdered by N'Jobu's son Killmonger, after offering himself for T'Challa's life.

Tabard decorated with beads, wood, and bones

A TERRIBLE SECRET

Zuri feels guilty for betraying T'Chaka's brother N'Jobu and abandoning his son N'Jadaka (Killmonger) in America. After T'Challa sees Killmonger's royal ring, Zuri finally confesses the truth.

DATA FILE

AFFILIATION: Wakanda, T'Chaka, T'Challa
KEY STRENGTHS: Loyalty to the royal family, self-sacrifice, knowledge of Wakandan lore
APPEARANCES:
Black Panther

Sleeves marked with Wakandan symbols

KEEPER OF THE HEART-SHAPED HERB

As a spiritual advisor and friend to the royal family, Zuri is trusted with many secrets. Among them is tending the cave of heart-shaped herbs that bestow the power of the Black Panther.

Ceremonial attire

Zuri oversees the Challenge Ceremony. He strips Prince T'Challa of the heart-shaped herb's power before the fight.

Crimson robe of leadership

EVERETT K. ROSS

CIA agent

Everett K. Ross is a CIA agent and Deputy Task Force Commander of the Joint Counter Terrorist Center, in charge of enforcing the Sokovia Accords. When Ross is shot during a scuffle with Ulysses Klaue and Killmonger, Nakia convinces T'Challa to take him to Wakanda for treatment. While there, Ross joins the fight against the usurper Killmonger.

Regulation CIA tie is just a little too tight

Expensive taste in watches

Always dressed in professional attire

Pocket contains communication device blocked in Wakanda

Ross must remote pilot a Wakandan airship to shoot down Killmonger's weapons shipments to other countries.

Folded arms reflect skeptical nature

THE WAKANDAN CONNECTION

While investigating events in Sokovia, Ross discovers that Ultron's vibranium came from Ulysses Klaue, which leads back to Wakanda. Ross first met T'Challa during the Avengers' Civil War. They meet again when they both pursue Klaue.

MASTER INTERROGATOR

Ross questions Ulysses Klaue after capturing him in South Korea. Klaue tells Ross that Wakanda is much more than it seems. The secretive nation is wealthy and technologically advanced.

DATA FILE

AFFILIATION: CIA, Sokovia Accords, Wakanda
KEY STRENGTHS: CIA and Air Force pilot training
APPEARANCES: Captain America: Civil War, Black Panther

T'CHAKA

Former King

King T'Chaka of Wakanda is the husband of Queen Ramonda and the father of Crown Prince T'Challa and Princess Shuri. After a devastating tragedy in Nigeria involving the Avengers and Wakandan aid workers, T'Chaka heads the Sokovia Accords—an effort to hold the Avengers accountable for their actions. A terrorist bombing ends his reign.

Gray hair from the heavy burdens of office

FATHER AND SON

T'Chaka and his son T'Challa love each other deeply. The two share a final moment of affection at the signing of the Sokovia Accords before a bomb blast tears them apart forever.

TERRIBLE SECRET

T'Chaka has to make difficult decisions, putting the good of his country before his own family. In an effort to keep Wakanda safe, he turns against his own brother, N'Jobu, and abandons his young nephew, N'Jadaka, in America. The boy grows up to become Killmonger.

Beard trimmed shorter than in T'Chaka's youth

Western-style attire for international audience

After receiving the heart-shaped herb, King T'Challa meets T'Chaka's spirit in a vision on the Ancestral Plain.

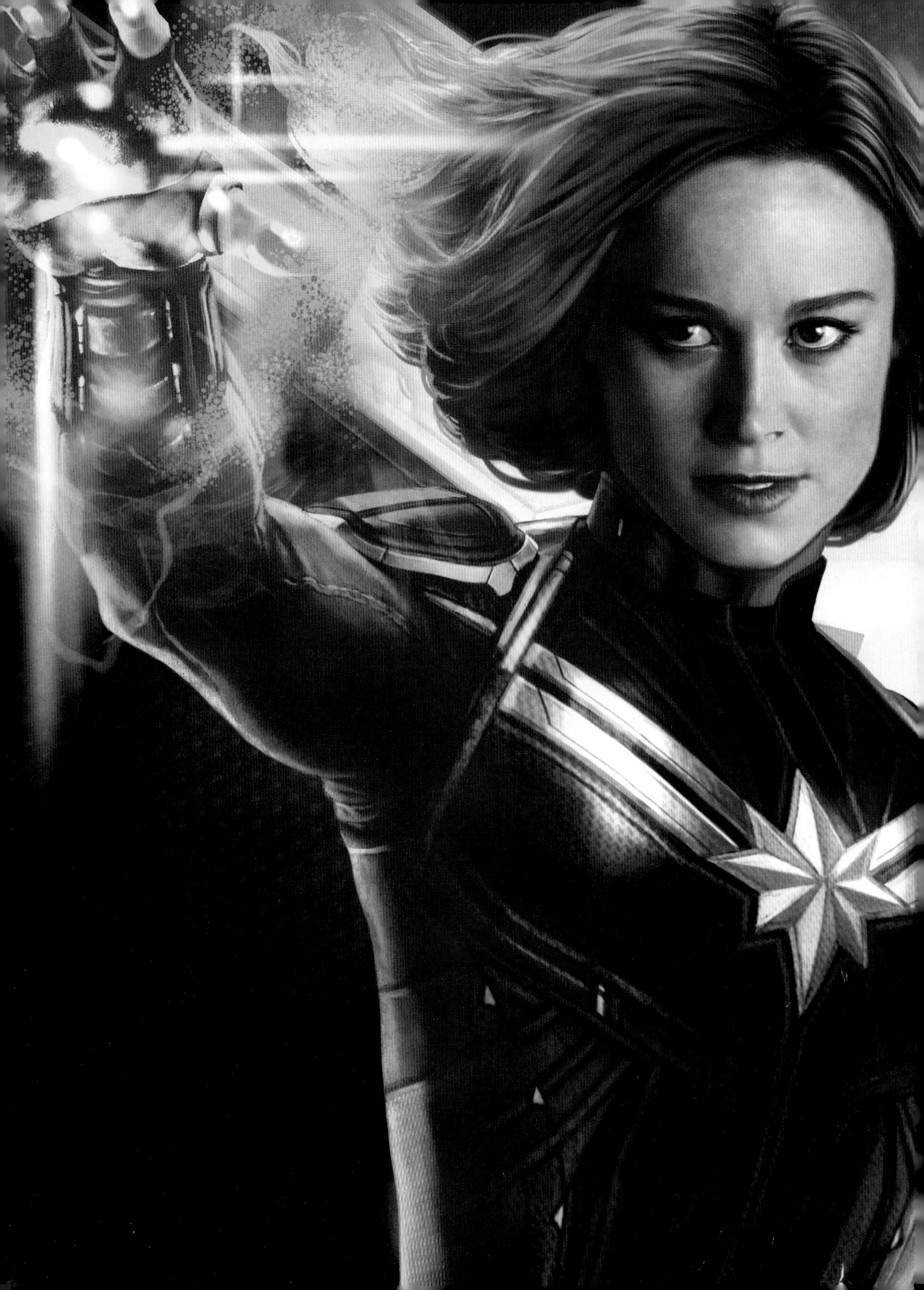

CAPTAIN MARVEL

Air Force pilot Carol Danvers becomes one of the galaxy's most powerful beings. Working with super spy Nick Fury, she fights to save Earth from a secret war between the Kree Empire and invading Skrull aliens.

CAPTAIN MARVEL
Cosmic-powered hero

Kree soldier Captain Marvel finds herself on planet Earth, with no knowledge of how she got there. She is tracked down by S.H.I.E.L.D. agent Nick Fury and begins to question whether her dreams and visions might be actual memories of the past. Marvel and Fury join forces, hoping to prevent an invasion of Earth by the dangerous, shapeshifting aliens, the Skrulls.

Starforce emblem

Suit protects against the pressures of space

PILOT PAST

Captain Marvel eventually remembers her past, in which she was a U.S. Air Force pilot named Carol Danvers. Danvers was a top pilot, with fast reflexes and exceptional courage.

Body able to absorb energy

STARFORCE

Captain Marvel is a member of the elite Kree military unit, Starforce. Marvel's photon powers make her a highly respected member of the team, although she faces a constant struggle to control her dangerous and unpredictable powers.

DATA FILE

AFFILIATION: U.S. Air Force, Starforce, Kree Empire, Nick Fury, S.H.I.E.L.D.

KEY STRENGTHS: Superior piloting abilities, enhanced durability, strength, and reflexes, cosmic energy blasts, healing abilities, space flight

APPEARANCES: Captain Marvel

Captain Marvel might be grappling with an identity crisis, but she remains dedicated to combating evil.

TALOS

Skrull spy

Talos is the ruthless leader of a group of Skrull aliens sent to spy on planet Earth. He is merciless, and feared even by those under his command. The Skrulls have waged a fierce battle against the alien Kree Empire for centuries, which brings Talos into conflict with Captain Marvel when they meet on Earth.

Pointed ears are an identifying Skrull trait

Green reptilian skin is the natural Skrull form

Skrull fabric is water- and bulletproof

Suit changes with body when shapeshifting occurs

SHAPESHIFTER

Skrulls are an invading alien race, known for their shapeshifting abilities. They can impersonate anyone they choose, which enables them to infiltrate the populations of planets they are planning to conquer.

A NEW TARGET

The Skrulls are a strategic, military-minded species. Before a full-on invasion, they send a team of spies to explore the territory and report back on its inhabitants.

DATA FILE

AFFILIATION: Skrulls
KEY STRENGTHS: shapeshifting ability, intelligence, military strategy, ruthlessness
APPEARANCES: Captain Marvel

INDEX

Main entries are in **bold**

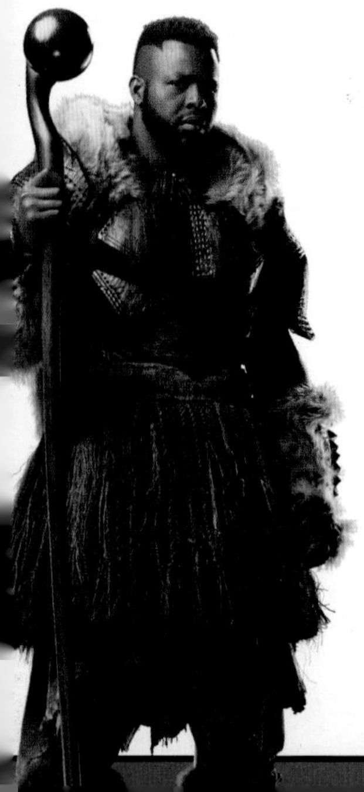

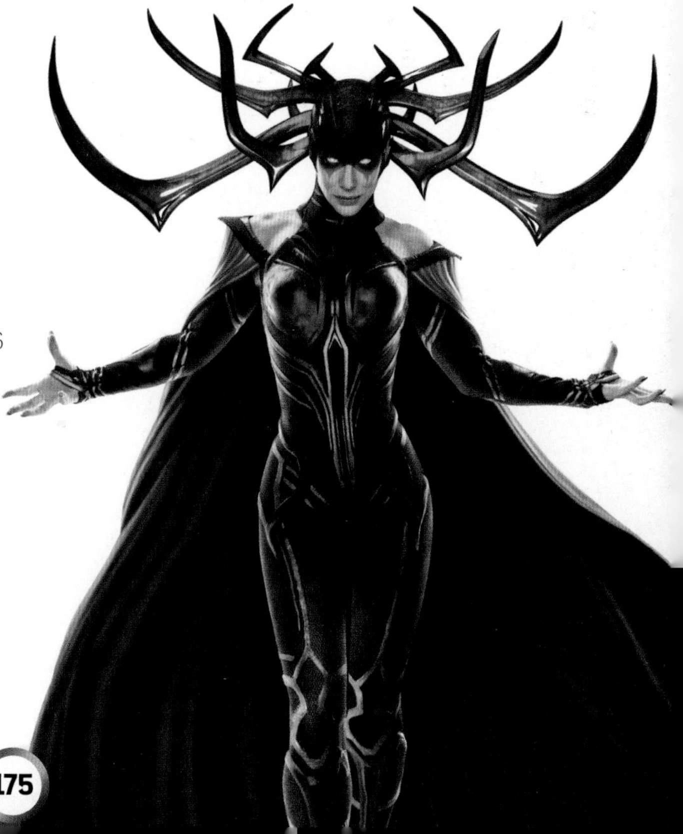

DK would like to thank Kevin Feige, Louis D'Esposito, Victoria Alonso,
Stephen Broussard, Eric Carroll, Craig Kyle, Jeremy Latcham, Nate Moore,
Jonathan Schwartz, Trinh Tran, Brad Winderbaum, Brian Chapek,
Mary Livanos, Zoie Nagelhout, Kevin Wright, Michelle Momplaisir,
Richie Palmer, Mitch Bell, David Grant, Dave Bushore, Sarah Beers,
Will Corona Pilgrim, Corinna Vistan, Ariel Gonzalez, Adam Davis,
Eleena Khamedoost, Cameron Ramsay, Kyle Quigley, Michele Blood,
Jacqueline Ryan, David Galluzzi, Ryan Potter, Erika Denton, Jeff Willis,
Randy McGowan, Bryan Parker, Percival Lanuza, Vince Garcia,
Matt Delmanowski, Alex Scharf, Jim Velasco, and Andrew Starbin at
Marvel Studios; Nick Fratto, Caitlin O'Connell, and Jeff Youngquist
at Marvel; and Chelsea Alon, Elana Cohen, Stephanie Everett, and Kurt
Hartman at Disney. DK would also like to thank Cefn Ridout for additional
editing, Megan Douglass for proofreading, and Helen Peters for the index.

AVAILABLE NOW ON VARIOUS FORMATS INCLUDING DIGITAL
WHERE APPLICABLE FOR THE FOLLOWING FILMS:
Iron Man, The Incredible Hulk, Iron Man 2, Thor, Captain
America: The First Avenger, Marvel's The Avengers, Iron
Man 3, Thor: The Dark World, Captain America: The Winter
Soldier, Guardians of the Galaxy, Avengers: Age of Ultron,
Ant-Man, Captain America: Civil War, Doctor Strange,
Guardians of the Galaxy Vol. 2, Thor: Ragnarok, Black
Panther, Marvel Studios' Avengers: Infinity War,
Ant-Man And The Wasp, Captain Marvel
© 2019 MARVEL

Project Editor Shari Last
Senior Designer Robert Perry
Designer Jess Tapolcai
Pre-Production Producer Marc Staples
Senior Producer Jonathan Wakeham
Managing Art Editor Vicky Short
Managing Editor Sadie Smith
Art Director Lisa Lanzarini
Publisher Julie Ferris
Publishing Director Simon Beecroft

First American Edition, 2019
Published in the United States by
DK Publishing
1450 Broadway, 8th Floor
New York, New York 10018

DK, a Division of Penguin Random House LLC
19 20 21 22 10 9 8 7 6 5 4 3 2 1
001–311499–April/2019

© 2019 MARVEL

Published in Great Britain by Dorling
Kindersley Limited

A catalog record for this book is
available from the Library of Congress.

ISBN: 978-1-4654-7889-4

DK books are available at special discounts
when purchased in bulk for sales promotions,
premiums, fund-raising, or educational use.
For details, contact:
DK Publishing Special Markets,
1450 Broadway, 8th Floor
New York, New York 10018
SpecialSales@dk.com

Printed and bound in China

A WORLD OF IDEAS:
SEE ALL THERE IS TO KNOW

www.dk.com
www.marvel.com

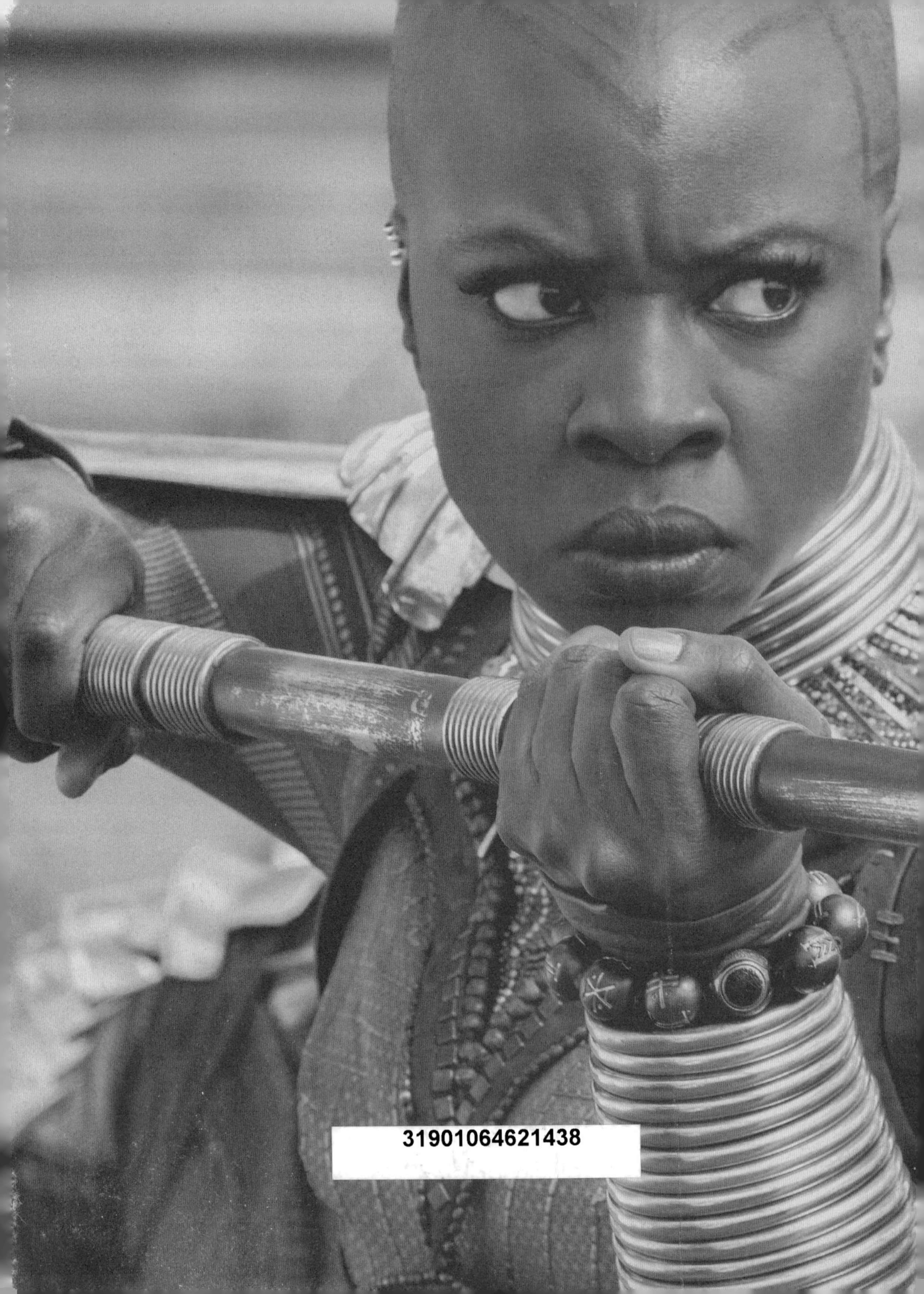